Also by Steven Key Meyers

Fiction

Save the Max Man!
A Family Romance
The Last Posse
Another's Fool
Junkie, Indiana
My Mad Russian
The Wedding on Big Bone Hill
Queer's Progress
All That Money
Good People

Non-Fiction

I Remember Caramoor: A Memoir

*The Man in the Balloon:
Harvey Joiner's Wondrous 1877*

Plays

*A Journal of the Plague Year,
and Other Plays and Adaptations*

Springtime in Siena

Two Short Novels

Steven Key Meyers

Springtime in Siena

Copyright © 2020 Steven Key Meyers
All Rights Reserved
ISBN 978-1-7330465-4-1
Published by Steven Key Meyers/The Smash-and-Grab Press

No part of this publication may be reproduced, stored in a retrieval system or transmitted in any form or by any means, electronic, mechanical, recording or otherwise, without the prior written permission of the author.

All characters appearing in this book are fictitious, and any resemblance to real persons, living or dead, is coincidental. A previous edition was published in somewhat different form under the title *New York / Siena* by BookLocker in 2012.

2020 First Edition

SMASH
&GRAB
press

Contents

Springtime in Siena   3

The Man Who Owned New York   93

Springtime in Siena

For Anne and Dan and Diana and Ginny

1.

STUDYING MY YOUNGER SELF as I might any artifact from a curious era (and we're talking Seventies!), I observe that although not bad to look at—handsome, in fact—he is of his time: slender, hirsute, given to queasy color combinations, eager to build a better world. So eager, in fact, that he pursues a teaching career straight into the heart of futility, from which he looks for consolation to—in the lingo of the day—"lifestyle." Hoping to glimpse a spark of promise, I place him under different lights and compare him to other exemplars, but can only shake my head. Ruefully but honestly, I'm forced to conclude: Not only is this person not *destined*, he is not even *eligible* for the future he covets; the future that in fact has turned out to be his—that is, mine.

Because in 1974 I managed to turn things around. At 28, I didn't matter. A junior member of the art history faculty at Adams U. in Washington, D.C., I felt distinctly talked-out and ready to vary my routine by heading up a semester's study abroad with 17 undergrads.

SPRINGTIME IN SIENA

It was during that sojourn in Siena, Italy, in the verdant springtime of my youth that I decided to count in the affairs of the world—to be someone who mattered. Under the tutelage first of a disastrous affair, and then by falling in love, I began to focus the scattered strands of self, to bend them in one coherent direction. I exerted my will, at a time—in the kingdom of love and peace—when that index of one's love of life was suspect. Through *will* I abandoned the lifestyle that debarred me from the world's respect; through *will* achieved the critical mass that's carried me through to where I am at the present day, pretty well known, I think, throughout the museum world.

This, then, is my memoir of how I grew up. I mean it neither as how-to guide nor celebration of ego, and if it's frank, it has to be.

Rest assured, no one was harmed in the writing of it.

2.

ON A JANUARY SUNDAY I rode a charter bus in solitary splendor from Siena, the city of 50,000 in central Tuscany where I'd established myself days earlier, to Florence to meet my *Springtime in Siena* group.

Before going to the train station I dashed through an exhibition at the *Uffizi* of Doré's illustrations to Dante. An Englishwoman was going around the walls with a younger man. She wondered aloud whether the voluptuous *Paolo and Francesca*—lovers condemned to circle each other, forever unable to touch—illustrated *l'Inferno* or *il Paradiso*.

"It's sexual," her companion learnedly lisped. "Must be the *Paradiso*."

Wrong!

Still laughing, I got to the *Stazione Termini* scant moments before my group's scheduled 2:00 o'clock arrival. The board in the waiting room told me at which *binario* its train would arrive. In the clangorous, glass-roofed shed I found the platform but no sign of the train, though gigantic steel springs at the tracks' end introduced an antic possibility of disaster. Plenty of people were waiting, among them a young man standing with the contrapposto stance and compressed energy of Michelangelo's *David*. Hips cocked, he peered alertly up the tracks, a day-pack slung at his shoulder, a bag leaning against his shin like Goliath's head. He wore, and wore well, Levis and a leather jacket.

Without willing it, I walked closer to this kid. Had nothing in mind save a vague desire to see if his face could be as sexy as the rest of him. I didn't know of any place we could go; I never patronized men's rooms. Possibly the station chapel? Except that in Italy a species of black-veiled widow tends to infest them. Besides, the train was due any moment.

Still, I was curious what he would do if I made my intentions — however fallacious — clear. So I took up my stance ten feet behind him and stared at his shaggy dark head.

The crowd milled, the pushcart vendor of *affreschi* bawled for trade, P.A. announcements overlaid one another incomprehensibly, on other tracks trains pulled in or pulled out — and within a minute Einstein's "spooky action at a distance" happened: My kid scratched his ear, swung around flipping hair off his handsome features and drilled fine brown eyes straight into mine.

My crotch knotted. I could see that he knew exactly what he wanted. In response I beetled my brow, thrust out my lip — glowered at him with that seeming disgust men use to signal interest in one another — and nodded towards the chapel. He lightly let down his pack — disarmed himself, as it were — showed his teeth and *laughed*.

My nod went spastic, and probably fear swamped my face, for only then did I recognize him: This was no willing pickup in that glorious dawn of gay self-respect, when youth joyously gave itself away. No, this was *Jack* somebody, an Adams U. junior who, I remembered too late, had planned to tour the Continent on his own before joining up with the group.

He laughed again, probably at the effort of lock-down clamping my jaws and reddening my cheeks. I hate being seen at a loss.

"*Ciao*, Jack," I said as we shook hands. Fortunately my voice had its usual crust of authority. "Or should I call you *Giacomo? Benvenuto in Italia.*"

"Hey, *professore.*"

"How were your travels?"

"Pretty hot," he began with a malicious grin.

Told him to hold the fort while I went to find a magazine.

I had a rule against sleeping with my students. It was a rule more honored in the breach than in the observance (no pun intended), since while I avoided those enrolled in my courses I made hay elsewhere in the student body. Not that my own students lost out: Though my performance in bed was generally congratulated, I know I was really at my best in the classroom.

In the waiting room, light washed off the travertine walls as I surveyed a magazine rack with the posture—entirely dissociating himself—of someone looking over a used car. For, shrouded in the chiaroscuro of a Caravaggio martyr, Richard Nixon peered out from the covers of TIME, *Newsweek, L'Espresso, Der Stern, The Economist*. He had the long nose of a liar and furtive eyes which sincerely wished to duck the issue. Watergate was more than six months away from working itself out, but its awesome end—*his* end—was inevitable. I was half sorry to find myself posted so far away as the moment of the kill approached, for I sensed it would end that dark period which started the afternoon Kennedy died and lasted through the corrosive adventure known as Viet Nam and give rise to new energies and opportunities.

Jack touched my shoulder.

"It's here."

"Super," I said. "Let's go face the music."

Buying TIME and *Newsweek*, I rolled them into a baton and marched to the platform—briskly, lest Jack say anything more.

3.

ONLY TWO MALES, Jack and Michael the Viet Nam vet, had enrolled in the group; for whatever reasons, Italy exerts a stronger attraction on American women than men. But on the platform the first thing I noticed was an unexpected but welcome extra boy standing tall and handsome among the girls. A last-minute addition? His open face, looking provocatively aside, reminded me of Donatello's *St. George* (whose features Michelangelo filched for his *David*).

But the last steps broke the spell, and I recognized Briana, one of our art history majors. Briana! Not Donatello after all, but Botticelli — *The Birth of Venus*' robust blossoming nude. Briana had a fine, strong figure (high-school field hockey champion, I later learned), good bones and a marvelous glow of health, what only the greatest masters achieve in giving their creations the semblance of life.

Gary — I said to myself — *it's not your style to undress the girls. What's going on?*

I greeted the women and then sorted out Michael. A combat veteran 23 years old, he was the group's elder. Dangerous red suffused his face as he glared at a vendor for what he dared sell his girlfriend, Katie: a styrofoam cup filled with *caffé* to the level of an inch.

"*Signore!*" Michael demanded, his ponytail bouncing in indignation as the vendor dealt with new customers. "*Uno momento!*"

Katie, a sapling-thin beauty with high cheekbones and perfect pallor, looked on with mournful doe's eyes. Why she was with us and not on the runways of Milan that were her ambition was a mystery. Obeying Daddy's precepts about getting an education first? Why she was with Michael and not someone more presentable was probably to make Daddy apoplectic.

"Hey, Michael," I said, "that passes for a full cup, believe it or not."

"He *cheated* us, he sees we're American and—"

"Taste it," I urged. "It's strong. Espresso. You wouldn't want more."

Michael held it out to Katie, she took a sip, and with a moralist's face—his brow bulging out beneath the absurd long hair—he awaited her judgment. People always exclaimed at his gentleness, but I knew he really wanted to kill us all.

Katie registered approval and Michael, relenting, rewarded me with a soul handshake (the rage then). And as I found was usual with him, he began to find things funny. Why not? He was Irony's favorite, caught by the draft at 18 a high-school dropout, now set to enjoy a semester in Italy as part of his architecture studies courtesy of the latest GI Bill.

His lady love smiled at him, and was about to smile at me when I abruptly turned around. Katie had been in my Impressionism class and I remembered her habit of commanding *"Smile!"* to anyone not already grinning like an idiot. But in the Seventies people did that. People would go up to serious-looking persons and say, *"Smile!"* Everybody felt they had to keep up the love-and-peace crap.

I herded the group to the coach through a sun-gilt plaza filled with burping motor scooters, shiny little cars and the plaints of flower sellers, the kids having to goose-step so as not to trip on their bellbottoms. (I was already outfitted with a new Italian wardrobe featuring slender-legged pants and sharp-toed shoes.)

Our bus moved down broad streets, crossed the Arno,

passed the Pitti Palace and swung onto the *Superstrada*. Landscape began to roll past in blurred textures woven by cultivation continuous since Etruscan times. Rows of grapevines writhed up worn hills to the ancient stone structures surmounting them, and brown thickets lined the valley watercourses. The mistiness that is the very element of Europe's atmosphere softened the glittering sunshine. As we sped towards them, the Chianti Hills appeared to levitate and become bruised clouds.

Enclosed by glass, made spectators of their own destinies again, as if they were watching TV, and with motion imparting a reassuring throb to their crotches, the kids began to relax. They made primping visits to the *gabinetto* in the rear and lounged back in their seats. Hairbrushes came out for elaborate repairs (it was Farrah Fawcett-Majors' heyday) and chatter arose as from a cocktail party at the second round of drinks.

Up the aisle, Michael huddled over Katie as she tried to wring warmth from her long fingers. Across from me Jack sat with his heels on the seat, clasping his knees and looking out the window. He'd taken off his jacket, and the bunched sleeve of his T-shirt revealed an untanned stretch of arm that looked remarkably nude. Then he slumped against the window and challenged me. I ignored him. Instead I turned the memory of my mistaken first sight of Briana this way and that, like a locket: *Me* responding to a *woman?* What was the meaning of *that?*

When we passed beneath Monteriggione, a fortified hill town for centuries at issue between Florence and Siena, I stood up, putatively to point it out, but really to get another glimpse of her. I had some difficulty distinguishing hers from the dozen other blonde heads until she turned her eyes from Monteriggione to me in what struck me, despite the Nordic quality of her beauty, as the Latin manner, the whole liquid eye arched and upward-aiming. I sat down again, much struck.

Siena presides over Tuscany from where three hills meet. Huge churches crown the lower two, while her cathedral—the *Duomo*—rises atop the highest. The city is built entirely of stone and ruddy brick. In the Middle Ages she parlayed her position on the *Via Francigena*—the pilgrim road to Rome—into wool and banking businesses, and vied with Florence for power and riches until 1348, when plague ravaged the Sienese while sparing (comparatively) the Florentines. Two centuries later Florence conquered Siena, finishing her as a force in history and flash-freezing her appearance in time.

Although Siena possesses magnificent views, she vouchsafes only fugitive glimpses of herself to those approaching; the swell of hills protects her. Her famous *Piazza del Campo* lies hidden in the center beneath the mighty *Torre del Mangia* that pierces the sky 300 feet overhead. As our bus moved effortlessly uphill, climbing past gas stations, garden plots, boxy villas, terra-cotta apartment houses, we could just see the travertine tip of the *Torre*'s finial. The weather began to change and the sky closed up as we reached *Porta Camollia* on the ancient city walls, where massive gates bleached white by time stood open (until after the First World War they closed every night). The bus rumbled through.

Inside the walls, we had a brief prospect of the whole weathered city rumpled like a quilt. Churches and towers sprang free from the dense fabric with a perspective somehow jammed, as in medieval illuminations that make a man tall as a steeple. A rent in the clouds dropped other-worldly light onto the green-and-white–striped marble *Duomo*, making its dome a fluted Oriental hat. Then the rent healed and rain began to fall.

— *SPRINGTIME IN SIENA* —

The coach lumbered down a narrow street and started to turn into the even narrower *vicola* where stood the ancient Donato family *palazzo*. As usual, Prof. Donato was to teach the group its local history course, and he and his wife were kindly laying on a light *collazione* while I handed out the rooming assignments.

But the bus could not turn the corner. Its side scraped. The kids drew back appalled as stone glazed with 800 years of soot swam up to their windows.

"*Madonna!*" said the driver through bared teeth. He reversed, but scraped again. "*Manacc'!*" he growled, a word so bad he didn't dare finish it.

An Alfa-Romeo Giulietta rushed us head on. Its driver leaned on the horn. The bus driver shrugged, cursed, sawed forwards and backwards. *Scrape!* The Giulietta's driver removed his sunglasses in an ineffably theatrical gesture. Our driver eloquently threw up his hands. The Giulietta jerked backwards out of sight, then its driver reappeared on foot and, cupping his hands (and getting wet), guided the bus. We shot free of the turn and the drivers exchanged friendly waves. The episode had just that combination of aggression and cooperation that to me is the hallmark of the Italian character.

Upstairs in the Donatos' apartment—the 30 rooms of the *palazzo* they were reduced to—I paired off the women in *pensioni* and with host families. From excitedly babbling about the flight to Luxembourg and the slow crawl over the Alps and the rigors of changing trains in Milan, they grew quiet and apprehensive, craning at the cold grandeur that surrounded them, at crystal chandeliers whose droplets of light seemed reluctant to fall; at gods leering from the ceiling; at Prof. Donato's gleaming, sculptural head. Especially they shrank from Signora Donato's surveillance through enormous glasses of the type also favored by Sophia Loren. Without protest they allowed me to see them to their taxis or, in the case of those assigned rooms in the *centro città*, hand them a map and point the way. Separated from the group, pushed out into the rain dragging their baggage, they went as to the slaughter, bellbottoms dragging on wet stone.

Jack and Michael I sent to the Soviet-style apartment complex in suburban Acquacalda where Adams U. men always lodged. Our landlady there had beds available in two rooms already occupied by single students, so both would have the benefit of an Italian roommate. One was a medical student and the other, a Communist, a student of economics. In the event, the Communist refused to room with an American. He made a scene when Jack came in with his friendly smile. The first solution tried was to exchange Jack for Michael, but Michael's Army fatigue jacket sparked a worse uproar.

Beds were reassigned, and Jack and Michael ended up together.

4.

I NEVER DID get out to Acquacalda to visit the boys. It would have meant a three-mile hike or a ride by *autobus municipale*, which was impossible. The concept of the queue never having reached Italy, getting on a bus it's every man for himself. A mass jams the doorway and more or less sticks there. One can pass through this palisade of elbows only by main force, and to push up the aisle is to run the gauntlet.

And by the time I bought my little red sports car, it seemed better not to visit. But Jack told me all about life with Michael.

The first morning, the frantic beating of his alarm clock awakened Jack to the sight of what at first he took to be a bell tolling. Then he recoiled from the penis swinging in his face as Michael rooted around for the clock. (Jack always insisted he found straight men sexually repugnant.)

The noise stopped. Jack turned over and went back to sleep.

Five minutes later his body seized to his landlady's *"Giacomo!"*

Too late—irretrievably awake—he realized she was addressing her eight-year-old son, not her new boarder. He stretched in the bed's appalling softness.

"*Ciaody*, brother man," said Michael. "This bother you?"

Jack passed his hand over his face, looked over, saw nothing amiss. Then he caught a whiff.

Michael, sitting nude on his bed against the wall, was smoking and also solving an itch in his pubic hair. His big chest had a flag tattooed upside-down over the heart. His sturdy limbs were hairy except where clothing rubbed them bare. In his present position his scrotum enveloped the shaft of his cock to form something resembling a cow's udder. (To me, Michael always resembled Ammannati's hideous *Neptune* in Florence's *Piazza della Signoria*.)

He offered the joint.

"No thanks," Jack said. "Isn't that dangerous over here?"

"Good stuff. *Great* stuff. Bought it on the train."

"But the police?"

"World's full of cops, man," Michael remarked, tuning his tape player's radio to tinny Italian rock.

Jack followed his eyes to a photograph livid with fading reds on the table between their beds. It showed Michael and half a dozen other soldiers standing against jungle foliage squirting peace signs in front of their bellies. An impatient hand had drawn crosses over several heads.

After a single Italian song, Michael pressed *Play* and Diana Ross and the Supremes sang *Baby Love*. He squeezed the radio to his ear as though he needed every word.

A passage from the diary Briana kept during her first weeks rooming with Katie might convey something of Siena's quality:

I woke up in an instant. It was dark. Had there been a noise? I reviewed the silence. No noise; only an urgent need to pee.

Katie's breaths came rapid but faint. She went to bed complaining bitterly about the lack of heating, but outside the sheets it was cold. I reached an arm through the frozen air and lifted the phosphorescent clock: 5:43 a.m. Having gone straight to bed upon arriving at the Pensione Rezzonica, *we'd slept twelve hours through.*

And the 24 or 48 hours before that were a blur, in memory inconsecutive, broken, nightmarish. Clearly my body had no idea what time it was.

I switched on the bedside lamp. Unfortunately its glow roused Katie. She sat up wide-eyed, looking uncomprehendingly at me.

"Sorry," I said. "I need to pee, and—"

"What time is it?"

"Quarter to six."

Katie turned over. I put on my robe and went down the hall to the closet that houses the toilet—whose dubious cleanliness I am determined not to notice. Then I carried my bath things to the room with the elevated tub (there's no shower) and pushed buttons on a wall device. There commenced a spitting, sizzling and booming I hoped wouldn't wake anybody. Finally a few inches of hot water dribbled into the tub. I tempered it with cold, got in, bathed. Soon I was dressed and plowing through my hair with the blow dryer (fortunately the converter works).

Then I found my key and crept out the pensione's double doors and down three flights of stone steps, each flight lighted for 20 seconds by the push of a button. Opening the street door, I stepped onto Via Santucci.

High overhead the sky was brightening, but little light seeped down to street level. A three-wheeled cart rasped past in an acrid cloud of oil. Across the way an open door big as a barn's disclosed a workspace where boxes lay on trestles. A man wrestled one outdoors, and dawn defined its ebony shape: a coffin! The fruit and flowers carved on the lid grabbed the light as he leaned it against the wall.

The next shop was a bakery. The smell alone was nourishing. I went inside, but found no one there. I heard speech in the back, though, including my first native "Mama mia!" A woman sprinkled with flour came out to fetch a tray.

"Pane?" I asked.

"Non c'é ancora." And more. Come back later, I gathered.

I started walking. The streets are incredibly narrow and, as it turned out, dark even in daylight. Soon I came upon a broader street lined by great stone buildings. In the distance, peddlers called; as conveyed and shaped by stone their voices sounded exotic.

Rosy brightness beaming at one turning, I proceeded down a ramp and with dreamlike surprise entered the Piazza del Campo, still dark beneath the glowing Torre del Mangia. This is the heart of the city—literally the heart, where it receives light and air and pumps them through the streets. It looks organic, too, as if a giant's drawn up his knees to make a space where a cat might choose to sleep (actual cats prowled the edges, detaching themselves from the shadows as pigeons *clucked awake). Travertine stripes ray uphill from the* Palazzo del Comune *and bricks lie like herringbones between them. Curving façades of* palazzi *with trefoil windows, many with restaurants on their ground floors, enclose the* Campo *in the shape of a scallop.*

*The few people crossing it seemed to encounter friends halfway and paused to chat. Pigeons flew zigzag, flashing in sunlight only to be quenched in shadow. As I crossed, climbing, people smiled at me—maybe because of my damp hair, blonde without the dark roots proudly borne by Italian women, or maybe because Siena in early morning startled me into engagement (I know I usually seem aloof). It was the delight of seeing the idea of Italy replaced by Italy itself. Some even said "*Buon giorno.*" I gave "*Buon giorno*" back.*

I climbed hills, reached the walls, got irredeemably lost as people went to work and children walked to school with satchels on their backs. Catching a glimpse of candle-flame piercing darkness inside a church with a façade of rough brick, I pulled my handkerchief over my head and went inside to pray that I might find my way back to Pensione Rezzonica.

Soon after walking on I found coffins standing against a wall, and had to laugh at how glad seeing them made me feel!

Katie stirred as I came in, warm raisin loaves in hand.

5.

OUR CLASSROOM WAS near the walls, in a former convent belonging to the *Università di Siena*, which, founded in 1240, happens to be Europe's second oldest. Though deftly modernized, the building retained its medieval soul. Our room was a wonderful whitewashed chamber with tiers of desks facing mine at the bottom. Above my back, windows of ancient bubbled glass framed views of the countryside.

Our first class was Monday at 10:00 a.m. sharp. The kids came in bright-faced and eager, already recovered from jet-lag — ready, I judged, to hear that I was on to them.

Accordingly, I told them that although their parents might think they were in Italy to study *art* — to swoon before old pictures, waxing lyrical about composition and impasto — I knew they were there for *sex*.

How they blushed!

It was ever thus, I assured them. And they'd come to the right place if they wanted to have affairs at comparatively little cost. Italy remains what it's been since Roman times, a theme park for losing one's innocence. They stamped out the last vestiges of it there eons ago.

That Americans, particularly young Americans, are innocent is, of course, our shrewd, self-serving national article of faith. It's an innocence jury-rigged, patched, repainted and put back on the road again so many times you have to wonder who we think we're fooling, but there it is: We Americans possess innocence, and we know it (never mind that innocence by definition is unaware of itself). We've also adopted its despised cousin, sincerity.

That's why, I remarked, they were "studying art." Their burdensome "innocence" demanded that it be "lost" in a locale sacred to such sham ceremonies, and Hollywood and English literature alike portray Italy as the ideal place to love and lose and generally loosen up. Endure the slaughter in the spirit of play, I suggested, and they would go home essentially intact, if virgins no longer.

They tittered, and I proceeded to snap through slides of *Quattrocento* pictures.

Soon enough things slipped into that deadly routine every semester takes on. Everybody found a groove.

Myself, I lucked into a diversion. By the second week I was fucking Jack.

6.

JACK WAS ENROLLED in an independent study course with me, as was Briana. Lacking an office, I scheduled them to come to my apartment on Via Roma, Jack at 3:00 o'clock Wednesdays, Briana at 4:00. There we could sit in my parlor with its view of the *Chiesa di San Francesco* looming over red tile roofs. That would give me something to look at while they droned on.

The first Wednesday, Jack and I simply kicked around some ideas. We sat on the antique settee, balancing on our knees a beautifully printed book on Giotto (to this day, Italians are the best printers). Our thighs exchanged warmth as I suggested he familiarize himself with Siena's own art, perhaps study how her painters treated a given theme through the centuries.

By our second meeting, he'd come up with a viable topic. I'd perfected my plan, too. After all, why not? I had no intention of forcing myself on him, but the pickings were slim in Siena. I was particularly put off by the band of queers that orbited the *Campo* afternoons and evenings.

"Something struck me, *professore*—" Jack started.

"Call me Gary," I murmured.

"Gary. I visited the *Pinacoteca* and saw a wonderful Mateo di Giovanni *Slaughter of the Innocents*. He's a local, right?"

"Sure."

"Plus there's a School of Lorenzetti, same subject. Then I went across to the *Duomo,* and on the floor's another Mateo di Giovanni *Slaughter,* incised in marble: babies being tossed on swords. *Amazing*. Then at the *Duomo* museum—"

"Duccio's *Maestà?*"

"One of its little panels is a *Slaughter,* a bloody one: Two guys holding baby boys by the heels put swords into them, while mothers plead and—"

"I know the piece."

"Looks like something from the natural history of lions. Anyway, I'd like to examine the genre."

"Sounds good," I said. "Be quite a project."

"That's OK."

"Fine, then. Study one or two a week, report back, we'll see what the local resonance is, if any."

And I stopped spouting nonsense and pounced.

Not my fault. Rules may be rules, but when in Rome. Jack was giving me every signal in the book. His legs were spread, his eyes beating a path to my crotch. What could I do? If he didn't want to, he could tell me all about it.

So I grabbed his knee. That widened his eyes and parted his lips. Before he could close them I was contending with his tongue for mastery.

Within moments clothes were flying.

"I want to fuck you," I growled, and over he went, up came his ass (it was a poem) and I primed us with lube. He was the *David* brought to earth, his anus no longer a little polished triangle bestowed by Michelangelo, but puckered and penetrable. I reared up and went to work. He pleaded something, but I paid no mind. My angry-looking cock's purity of form claimed my attention as I withdrew it only to pound it home again. A mirror would have been great. I know I looked good.

It was time. I was ready. I thrust, and thrust again.

The doorbell rang.

Jack moaned the protest orgasm always extorts and a rope of white uncoiled to the side.

The doorbell rang again. My watch said 3:50. I withdrew, wiped myself and yelled, *"Coming!"* (mentally adding, "I *wish"*). With Superman speed I dressed myself from garments on the floor and threw Jack's, with Jack, into the bathroom.

As soon as its door closed I opened the front one.

Briana stood there with a look of surprise, gripping her bookbag defensively.

"Hi there," I said. "Right on time. I'm afraid Jack and I went over."

She stepped in and did one of those comprehensive looks around that women do. The toilet flushed.

"Jack's still here?"

"Just leaving," I said, and there he came. He was blushing, dammit, but dressed and flinging back his fringe.

"Hey, Briana."

"Hey, Jack."

He left with a handshake, a secret flicker of eyelashes and a hearty, "Great class, *professore*."

I closed the door on his laughter. Briana revolved once more before she decided to sit down and take out her notebook, crossing one bellbottom over the other. Her nostrils flared from time to time. Sex creates a quality in a room, no doubt about it, but one hard to place for what it is—not so much a scent or sight as a residue of mood, an impalpable airborne tumescence, a slow snapping away into nothingness of energies that are spendable in one way only.

It was a cinch that Briana was a virgin and had no accurate idea of what was agitating her. What was agitating *me* was unique in my experience. As if naturally I held a throw pillow to my lap. That pillow was hiding my erection! It's true I hadn't been satisfied, but the normal ebb, so uncomfortable when there's been no release, did not occur. Briana sat in an armchair opposite me with all propriety, while dirty, dirty thoughts coursed through my head: What would kissing her be like? What did her breasts feel like? What did her legs look like spread open?

My cock wanted to test that body until it found a place receptive to it, a place that yielded. It particularly wanted to root around between her legs. Never before had it wished such a thing!

She'd already told me she wanted to study the *Madonna col Bambino*—Mary holding the infant Jesus on her lap, the single most common subject of Italian painting. I'd suggested the difficulty of turning up anything new in such well-plowed ground, that she should see what Siena had to offer in the way of inspiring another topic.

"I went to see Duccio's *Maestà*," she now reported defiantly. "Stood in front of it for an hour, *Professore*—couldn't move. *Everything's* there. I want to examine it as an archetype of the *Madonna col Bambino* theme."

That seemed more promising. The *Maestà* is indeed a mighty, mighty picture. Painted ca. 1308-1311 as the *Duomo*'s altarpiece, it assembles angels, prophets and martyrs against a dimensionless gold ground surrounding an enthroned, star-spangled Mary with the Infant at her breast. Originally its *verso* was painted in smaller scenes, but bold work with a saw long ago separated the two surfaces and split up the back into dozens of pictures, among them the little *Slaughter of the Innocents* Jack spoke of.

"So do *you* want to be a mother?" I hazarded as we were wrapping up.

I'd thought her eyes open before, but now they widened.

"I'm a feminist," she said (a half-daring admission then). "But oh yes. I've never told anybody that before," she added.

"That you're a feminist?" I needled. "Your secret's safe with me." After a respectful moment I added, "I'm honored."

7.

OUR TIME FOR SEX was the siesta, that marvelous Mediterranean institution whereby one eats lunch, gets drowsy, gives in and falls asleep. Americans resist, go back to work tired and snappish; our Protestant ethic demands it. But Catholicism sometimes (if erratically) takes more accurate account of human nature.

Jack usually ate lunch at the student *Mensa* in the crypt of *Sant'Agostino*, I most often at Bar Costa in the *Campo,* or rather, if the sun were strong enough, at a table out front. Afterwards we would meet atop my towering staircase and have at it before succumbing to sleep. We would wake up for round two, dress and get on with the day. Later, in the purple shadows of early evening, we might hail each other in the *passeggiatta,* wherein the townspeople throng up and down Via di Città at the close of the day—even traverse a stretch together, arm-in-arm by way of camouflage, for in Italy it's customary for young men to promenade thus; *not* doing so draws notice. At night Jack would sleep in his own innocent bed, which worked out well since sleeping with anyone gives me bad dreams.

But my position as teacher fucking his student was a vulnerable one. To allay suspicion we needed a blind.

And the perfect blind—one that misled everybody into coupling Jack with *Briana*—came about as a result of a suggestion Michael made over dinner one day at the *Mensa*.

If upstairs *Sant'Agostino* was heaven (a serene Perugino *Crucifixion* floats over the altar), its crypt—the *Mensa*—resembled Hell. Michael nailed it by comparing it to Piranese's prison etchings. In a cruciform space matching that upstairs, everything ecclesiastical had been replaced by things of the kitchen and the whole painted gray, except for some old fresco heads bobbing near the ceiling. It resounded with the sounds of infernal machines manned by sullen 30-year-old students (the kind eager to tell you Americans never grow up) shifting cigarettes at the corners of their mouths. Nave and transept were given over to tables and chairs; cigarette smoke boiled up like incense. The din was terrific. Everybody had to shout.

On this particular evening when Jack hefted his tray into

the echoing blast, Michael the genial host waved and yelled, "*Yo!* Dude!"

Jack joined him and Katie and Briana—they sat in the same row in class, too—and bent beneath the noise to catch Michael's crazy riff. He was always holding forth; come in at "Man, it's all about marketing," you went out to "That's corporate bureaucracy, man."

He was telling them about Woodstock.

"Love and peace? More like people freaking out. Not generally known, but one night the state troopers started shooting? Let me put it this way: Not half a mile from the stage at Woodstock, you'll find the mass grave—*if* you care to look. But that's all I'm saying."

Jack and Briana conscientiously twirled their spaghetti.

Katie, too, returned to her food. She ate sparingly but with concentration, watched with bated breath by a coterie of admirers. They gathered at every meal—Italians, Greeks, Israelis, Palestinians—to watch the spectacle, the first tier turning their chairs around, the second sitting on tables, the rest standing behind. Periodically they stretched out their arms to flick off cigarette ash.

Katie's beauty was what drew them, but they were also fascinated by the way she treated food as the enemy, by her bite-to-bite combat with it. High protein was her mantra; pasta never passed her lips. She lived on nibbles of *Bistecca Fiorentina*, half-spoonfuls of yogurt. She would spend five minutes carving a lean morsel of beef even leaner. Such attitudes are foreign to Italy—in fact, carry a shiver of sacrilege, even of witchcraft.

The men would watch until she spilled the cold remains of her meal into a plastic UPIM bag and departed with Michael to dump it tenderly near the *Campo* for the cats. Her coterie broke up then, stepping on butts and shrugging their shoulders.

Finally Michael snapped out of it.

"Hey, guys," he said, "Katie and I are hitchhiking to Urbino this weekend, maybe even Ravenna. Like to come along?"

"The ducal palace is famous," Katie put in.

Jack and Briana exchanged glances. I envision her at that moment like Mary in Leonardo's *Annunciation*, hand to breast in astonished *"Me?"* but eyes already shining with the courage to see it through.

"How would we work it?" she asked.

And Michael, who'd hitched the States with a dog-eared Kerouac in his pocket, explained his scheme of traveling by couples and linking up at prearranged times and places.

"You ladies will look like goddesses beside the road. Only a *finochio* would stop for Jack or me." *Finochio* means faggot. "We should take advantage while we're in country."

"I will if you will," Briana told Jack.

"Do you good, man," Michael offered.

He was probably pitying Jack's solitary evenings. His own he spent at *Pensione Rezzonica* massaging Katie's delicate vertebrae until in no uncertain terms her landlady told him to go home.

8.

JACK AND BRIANA agreeing to the Urbino scheme, they tried it the following Friday (we had no Friday classes).

He told me about it in lyrical detail.

Early that morning the four musketeers walked out of Siena through *Porta Pispini*. Mist clung to the trees as they descended to their eastward road, and fog evened out the hills that rolled to the horizon. The February countryside varied between a thin green and rich browns.

Then there was only the road, narrow and shoulderless, where the occasional car came zipping along, sprightly low Lancias or sleek new Alfa Suds or upright Fiats.

At the buzz of a motor Katie nestled backwards against Michael and launched her fabulous smile. For a moment Michael looked unaccountably sad as his left hand pulled her close and his right hand lifted, thumb high. The car, a Fiat 500, stopped. After preliminary parley (which gave him a chance to assess the driver's sobriety), Michael burrowed into its backseat, Katie sat down in front and, waving to their friends, they were borne away.

"That was easy," said Briana.

"Michael looked like a fetus in a jar," Jack noted.

Then it was their turn. Another Fiat 500 beetled near. They were fighting stage fright as they stepped forward, extended their thumbs, smiled. The car overshot them, but stopped and backed up with the whine of a fussing child. In back, Jack's chin rested on his knees, but the roof was high enough, the sides glassy enough that he didn't suffer the claustrophobia an American coupe's backseat can induce. That model was then the mainstay of the Italian road, a tiny aerodynamic droplet fondly nicknamed *Topolino* — "Mickey Mouse" — whose two-cylinder engine produced upwards of 18 peppy horsepower.

So it went all day. They progressed with rides of five or ten kilometers. A lull might beach them on the roadside for an interval, but they were equally beached, happy to take in the exquisite aspects of landscape and weather. Then a car would approach, they appealed to it—following Michael's advice to stand where a driver could easily pull off, to make eye contact, to smile—and either it stopped for them or another one soon did. We say youth's a time of open-ended possibility, which makes it an illusion even for the young, but one very good thing about it is the willingness to enjoy delightful things that come at random.

Not only was it a heady experience to point at the countryside ahead and so obtain the means of getting there, it meant a quantum leap with their Italian. Needing to communicate with individual Italians who were warm and inquisitive, they began to speak the language. It was more than weeks of living in Siena had enabled them to do.

For lunch they bought loaves dusted with flour, cheese, *mortadella*, oranges, tasty Italian beer, and feasted beneath an olive tree.

North of Perugia (where they made a lightning tour of cathedral and square), as the day waned they entered a narrow valley bounded by steep green hills that churned clouds between them. Cypresses stood sentry over farm buildings, while bell towers served somehow to regulate the scene. An hour before sunset they were dropped at the Urbino turnoff, at the base of a road the map showed switching back on itself again and again, and waited beside a many-armed sign. Light traveling flat beneath the lid of clouds smacked them in the face and transfigured the countryside to green and gold. Traffic ceased. They began to worry.

Finally a Lancia stopped and shot them uphill. A young man in a hurry drove it, his girlfriend beside him. He accelerated urgently into every curve, making the rosary and *corne* hanging from the mirror rattle against each other *(corne* are phallic twists of coral, sovereign against the Italian malady of the evil eye). A turn brought a view of Urbino glowing in the last of the sun, a hilltop mass of red stone. By the time they charged up to the gates, it was pitch-black, and nowhere was there any sign of Katie or Michael.

They found a hotel. The proprietress asked, *"Siete sposati?"* ("Are you married?") "No," Jack replied, Lord knows why. *"Fidanzati?"* she asked. ("Engaged?") "No."

She asked no more questions, but gave them a room.

Next door, Jack and Briana found a *trattoria* whose brick oven produced intensely flavorful pizza. After eating they returned to their hotel and, rather solemnly, got ready for bed.

Their room had a *letto matrimoniale*, a table, a chair and a faulty door to a toilet. They permitted each other to undress unseen, perform ablutions unremarked upon, heave without consequences into bed. They fell asleep with no exchange of touch or words (aside from a stilted *"Buona notte")* or smells or emissions, or anything but one electrifying if accidental brush of the feet.

At what point of that day (or night) Briana began to fall in love with Jack, I don't know. But given her difficult, essentially fatherless upbringing, I think it natural not only that her first shared experience with a man should result in her falling in love with him, but that she would assume he felt the same towards her and not realize how he might take advantage.

9.

THAT WAS A DAY of settled cold rain back in Siena. Rain was still ringing down on the stone streets with terrific authority that evening when I found my way to *La Lizza*. I was horny.

La Lizza is the formal park that lies beneath the fortress Florence built after finally crushing Siena, the *Fortezza Medicea*. Its purpose was not to repel invaders, but to keep the Sienese obedient to their Florentine masters on pain of instant vaporization. An immense crystalline structure of brick, the *Fortezza* rises atop a flattened hilltop within shelling distance of the *Duomo* and everything else inside the walls. Sixteenth-century cannon still aim their dragon mouths at the city.

Beneath the looming mass, the park's terraces embrace fenced-off trees, benches and urinals that, in the Continental manner, shield users from knee to shoulder. It is Siena's pick-up place. I'd innocently come upon it on my first exploration of the city, found men there walking about giving each other hard looks. But I didn't wish to become known as a denizen; this was my first visit since.

A hardy few stood beneath umbrellas giving me hopeful glances as I walked past. I glowered at one of the younger ones — a kid with the blond Afro of a Botticelli angel — and we found a dry, secluded niche in the walls. But the results were not satisfactory. He was kissy, but his breath stank, nor was he as clean as an uncircumcised man should be. I offered myself half-masted — by no means my usual style — but soon broke away and zipped up. He spat idioms I wished I could understand as I hurried homeward.

Home was a quarter-hour walk across town, at the top of

the steepest staircase in the world—stairs you had to take a deep breath before committing yourself to. I chugged up them and opened my flat's oaken door with its blunt key.

First I closed the bathroom window's heavy shutters and started the wall-mounted water heater gushing and gurgling into the tub. Siena's winter cold was eating into my bones. Though by the thermometer nothing extreme—temperatures hovered in the 40s Fahrenheit—it was moist, and within the walls the ancient shadows seemed to intensify the cold until it was *frigid*. Because the apartment lacked heat except for what a space heater spat out through red-hot fangs, the bathroom—big and square, its fixtures (including a bidet) arranged around the walls—was the only room where, by virtue of filling the tub, I could get warm. I was spending a lot of time in there.

I took a *birra* from the fridge, put together *panini* of bread, salami and a local *formaggio,* carried them in with the latest TIME and treated myself to a soak. Ate my snack and caught up with the news from America (it was like reading about Mars). Finally I put my magazines aside, drained the great iron tub, refilled it and thought about what I'd gotten myself into.

It wasn't to win points with my colleagues that I'd volunteered to lead this semester abroad, but to get out of Washington for a spell to think.

Sick and tired of the sound of my own voice, in my fourth year of teaching I was certain I'd made a mistake in entering the profession. To bury myself in other people's art, snap endlessly through slides for kids snapping gum who'd rather be elsewhere—dreary, *dreary!* And I was expected to push my way up, dislodge somebody in a field that like every academic field was filled to overflowing by that doughty generation seared into immortality by World War II.

Regret is common to teachers, for teaching soon enough

shows itself to be a mug's game: You give everything you've got to those who don't want it, and for good measure society scorns your status, matches it with a risible salary and, truth be told, scorns your work itself. It's the right game for those whose idealism can sustain dead classroom hours, dead hours grading papers, dead committee meetings; idealism or unintelligence or lack of initiative or fear of life unsheltered outside school. But wrong for the rest of us.

I turned off the tap and sank until water lapped at the overflow drain and offered to enter my mouth.

TIME spoke of the upcoming indictments of Nixon's henchmen Haldeman and Ehrlichman. Closer and closer; the inevitability was majestic. The time it was taking to kick out a dirty American President stamped it as an august event.

It was time to be taken advantage of for adjustment. Nixon's going, besides terminating American interest in Viet Nam (I knew any treaty we signed wouldn't be worth the paper it was written on), would present opportunities for those inclined to go for it. OPEC had just cut off oil to the United States and jacked up the price to the rest of the world, and the Club of Rome was declaring world resources to be nearly exhausted. The smart money had the USA at its last gasp, poised to revert to comparative powerlessness, even a new Dark Ages; but the smart money can be pretty dumb.

So did I want to keep on keeping on? Teaching the Jacks and Brianas? Fucking some of the Jacks? I felt a certain shame concerning Jack—shame of the shooting-fish-in-a-barrel variety. Sleep with students the rest of my life?

As an undergraduate I'd had flings with a couple of my own professors, dallied enough with a third to secure (finally only at the cost of a French kiss) a crucial fellowship. I regretted those affairs, but was that young I'd found my teachers impossible to resist. They took advantage of my inability to say no—exactly what they habitually counted on. If in memory I despised them, I despised my own youthful weakness more.

But wasn't my involvement with Jack—any man, for that matter—still youthful weakness? A naïve extension of boyhood's mateyness into a time when I'd be better advised to give up the things of a child, emancipate myself from the comfortingly familiar and face the world with a partner it would applaud? Could I not survive in the wider world like other people, out where the real prizes are plucked? Not the pretend rewards of the winkingly tolerant academy—the tenure, the committee chairs—but the money and power and respect? In other words, couldn't I as well as anyone marry a woman, be accepted as a contestant, give my ambition full rein?

If not, why not? Because I was in thrall to student cock?

But give up cock for cunt? I imagined touching one, stroking its lips, probing the saline deeps, making its fold the plinth for my erection... I was thinking of Briana and getting hard! Passing my hand over the soap, trying to sustain the fantasy, I began to squeeze myself raw.

10.

THE QUARTET'S ACCOUNT of their adventures dominated class on Monday. They'd met up accidentally at *St. Appollinaire in Classe* near Ravenna, when Jack and Briana came out goggle-eyed at its late Roman mosaics just as Michael and Katie stepped out of a plush Mercedes 18-wheeler. The driver, a homeward-bound Iranian, had taken one look at Katie and said, "Come with me to Persepolis."

"We were tempted," Michael reported. "Almost did it."

They returned to Siena late Sunday by train. I said I thought the train a comedown.

Almost every weekend after that, the foursome would *fare l'autostop*—walk out of town through one or another of the arched gates that present views of the countryside like Renaissance altarpieces, take up their stances and unfurl their thumbs. And their thumbs got them where they wanted to go, to Pienza, Assisi, Ancona, Venice, Arezzo, Elba, Lucca, Pisa, Viareggio (beneath the Carrara marble quarries that make the hills look snow-capped) and Orvieto (arriving at its hilltop *Duomo* at sunset, the mosaic façade magically aglitter). And not only did people give them rides, often they fed them, even put them up on the living-room floor.

Hitchhiking cost nothing, of course, but everything in Italy was cheap then; not as fairy-tale cheap as in the Fifties or Sixties, but cheap. Jack, for instance, received a monthly $150 from his parents—a pittance even in those days. But since the program covered his lodging, his expenses were few. A meal at the student *Mensa* cost a dollar or less, a decent restaurant $2 or $3. Hotels ran to $3 or $4 a night, student hostels half that. Movies were about $1; even clothing cost little once they got used to bargaining in the open-air markets.

And exchanging dollars on the road produced better rates

than at our historic bank, Monte dei Paschi di Siena, where I had an account. When I needed cash, I would enter its grand *palazzo* and, by dint of applying pressure for a quarter-hour to the crush of customers in front of me, arrive at the teller and hand over my bankbook, whose accordion pages he would unfold and, in the neat hand devised long ago for recording just such transactions, inscribe my withdrawal, converted at a rate between 540 and 620 *lire* to the dollar. Jack reported that, seeking out deals on the docks in port towns, Michael hovering protectively at his side, he got up to 780 *lire*.

But the most rewarding thing about hitchhiking, Jack told me, was how *alive* it made him feel—more even than sex, he claimed with a glint in his eyes. Hitchhiking called on energy and awareness, required a constant totting up of probabilities while demanding openness to every possibility, allowed him to see memorable sights in an interesting manner. By placing him squarely in the moment (not that this was the phrase in those days), hitchhiking made him a participant in the national life.

"But isn't it scary, getting in all those strange cars?" I asked.

"With a Madonna on every dashboard?"

The girls began to throw around *Jack and Briana* as if they were an item—a little jealously, too, although most of the others rapidly found local boyfriends. Twelve of those girls go unmentioned in this memoir, which reflects less authorial strategy than, alas, authorial memory lapse. Wasn't there a Caroline? And a Leslie? They were nice girls, game and uncomplaining when it didn't have to be that way; my colleagues had regaled me with stories of the "*P.U.!*" brigades they'd had to baby-sit. No, my group's encounters with Turkish toilets—holes in the floor equipped with slimy hand-grips—left them laughing. And no one got pregnant, thank

God, probably thanks to Departmental advice that even virgins should get themselves on the Pill before stepping foot in Italy.

His travels helped Jack find more *Slaughters,* among them Ghirlandaio's, Guido Reni's, Fra Angelico's, Giotto's, Raphael's, Castello's, bloody scenes dutifully invested with what he discerned were the required elements: King Herod looking on from on high; soldiers ripping babies from their mothers' arms and plunging swords into them; dead infants piling up against a background of classical architecture. He took his notes and bought his postcards.

Siena's own Mateo di Giovanni (ca. 1430-1495) produced no fewer than four versions. The best is a pretty fresco with a pressed-flower quality: While noble spectators watch from on high, mothers weep as men skewer their infants and discard them on the terrazzo. In the medieval manner, power is depicted as descending a vertical axis from King Herod down through the noble onlookers, the killers and mothers to the dead littering the floor. The scene's creamy classicism to an extent controls the chaos; window lattices assimilate the swords' diagonals, for instance, subordinating their lethality to a decorative motif.

Jack also acquired a poster of the *Uffizi*'s big, splashy *Strage degli Innocenti* by Daniele di Volterra (1509-1566), known as *Il Braghettone*. For my benefit he unrolled it, his face going sour.

"But I know this picture!" I said. "Always did like it. Sticks with you. Tell me about it."

"But it's *terrible*," protested Jack. "Frenzied. Abstract. He has his shapes, his brushstrokes, his glossy sculpturesque groups, but where does he realize babies are *dying?* The polish amounts to a kind of blur effect—a visual correlative of denial. He doesn't want you asking questions, it's too highly finished for that. It revolts me."

"Know why he's called *Il Braghettone*? 'Breeches-maker'?"
"No idea."
"Vasari named him that after he took the Vatican commission to cover up the nudity of Michelangelo's *Last Judgment* in the Sistine Chapel. Those loincloths snapping in the wind? Daniele's work."

His face twisted. I liked it.

"Maybe you could do a paper on Michelangelo's penises?" I suggested. "Compare and contrast with that derisively small one he gave Adam? Could probably get at *The Last Judgment*'s with X-rays — *if* you spend a lifetime ingratiating yourself with the Vatican."

He snorted. Very cute.

Sexually this was a gratifying time: Four days a week I went to bed with a sexy kid. The other three I tried new restaurants or drove out into the countryside in my Fiat Spyder, even happened into adventures on the side.

However discreet Jack was within the group (to my relief, be it said), back home he was a mainstay of the Gay and Lesbian Student Association. He attended — even chaired — its meetings, mediated between its factions, manned the recruiting table at registration, did yeoman's service decorating Hoover Hall for the monthly mixers.

That Jack was a proud gay man who liked it up the ass was Gay Liberation's gift. (He told me he was a top, too, but I took his word for it.) Men fucking men (white men, anyway) was a new thing then. My own student days were full of marathon handjobs, strenuous blowjobs, endurance bouts of frottage. Fucking represented something of a frontier, but I found it more pleasurable than any other act. As for the alleged inelegance of ass-fucking? Since wherever a man ejaculates is a kind of toilet, in fact elegance inheres to doing it in the gut.

Jack had settled into a pattern: Meet someone at a dance or

meeting, go home with him and enjoy a two or three weeks' affair that inspired neither to thoughts of love and which petered out without rancor or recrimination in a tacit mutual observance of waning novelty, when each would go in search of someone new.

He had a lot of experience for someone his age, nor would I have taken him to bed if he hadn't, for I didn't want him to complicate life by falling in love with me. I told him so early on, and he willingly agreed, even looked put out that I felt the need to be explicit: No strings. Jack was on to himself.

Or so we thought. He began to change. He began to cling. Attachment was not what I wanted. What I wanted was to fuck him in the ass.

11.

I HAPPENED TO SIT IN on Prof. Donato's class the mid-March morning he lectured on Florence's conquest of Siena in 1555.

As I walked up to the building, the kids were lingering in the sun. Katie sat on the bench beside the doorway in the penumbra of the umbrella she used as a parasol. It gave her a black halo, as it were, that allowed her face's bone structure to emerge as it didn't in the ordinary light of day. She really was beautiful; too lovely to have to wonder (as Jack told me she constantly did) what *she* had to say to the camera. The photographs the kids took of one another revealed a woman you'd swear was her glamorous cousin. On glossy paper Katie had major bones and eyes, perfect hair and skin, lips plumped to bursting. The camera loved that face; what it craved, I suspect, was precisely its blankness.

Whether Michael (hulking beside his alabaster goddess, smoking Marlboros) was the protector of the pretty girl in the flesh or of the ravishing creature on photo paper was never clear to me. She might have relieved his tension, but evidently her preference was for chastity. In two months, Briana told Jack, Michael's nightly massage of Katie's back had progressed to his occasionally rubbing a foot as well. It may be that she knew no more of their intimate lives than she did of Jack's, but Michael was always, with Katie, adoring and gloomy.

I greeted them and Katie, blinking eyelids iced like a child's birthday cake (yellow-green hues were the fad), shot me a smile meant to be contagious.

In the classroom we settled in while Donato harrumphed over his notes. I quite enjoyed his cultivated, extremely European lectures, reading from books and yellowed notes, making no concession to anyone's Italian or lack thereof. But the kids complained. They arrived in Italy barely able to say hello, but Donato lectured to them as he would to his Italian students, seldom essaying eye contact as he spoke in language limpid, musical and almost incomprehensible (Siena's aspirative dialect, which converts *c*'s to *h*'s and sounds almost Spanish, is considered the purest in Italy). He was too distinguished, descended from too many popes, to try and interest them. How could he be expected to care for our mongrel breed when his cousin was a count?

Of course the result was that the kids missed his account of Siena's early history, its Etruscan and Roman origins and the birth of her rivalry with Florence, even his monotone presentation (but he kept his composure only with difficulty) of the 1348 plague, which killed four out of five Sienese and froze construction of a new cathedral so enormous—three towering piers alone survive—the *Duomo* would have served merely as its transept.

But this morning it turned out everybody was able to follow as he related how Florence, determined to subdue its rival once and for all, in 1554 enlisted the aid of Emperor Charles V's Spanish armies. Besieging Siena, over the winter they starved its population of 40,000 until only 8,000 survived. That spring, at almost the last gasp, the Sienese did a desperate thing: They expelled those of her occupants incapable of bearing arms—the *bocche inutili*, "useless mouths"—that the rest might carry on the fight that much longer. Accordingly, one day in April 1555 they opened the gates of *Porta Fontebranda* and drove out 5,000 old women, old men, cripples and *children*—some 250 younger than *ten*—onto the waiting Spanish swords.

Donato opened *Il Diario delle cose avvenute in Siena dal 20 Luglio 1550 al 28 Giugno 1555* and read Alessandro Sozzini's eyewitness account of the resulting massacre, how he heard the

> strida e lamenti. Era la più gran compassione a veder quei putti svaligiati, feriti e percossi in terra a diacere, che averiano fatto piangere un Nerone; ed io avrei pagati venti-cinque scudi a non averli visti; chè per trè giorni non possevo mangiare ne bere che prò me facesse.

Heard, that is, the

> screams and cries, saw the pitifullest sight of those babies slaughtered, run through and dashed to earth.

> *It would have made a Nero cry; and for myself, I would have paid 25 scudi not to have seen this sight that meant I couldn't eat or drink for three days, except that they made me.*

Michael emitted a disturbed—and disturbing—cry. He hadn't sat still during Donato's lecture, but boiled, heaved, tossed. He'd fling a foot aside, then anchor it on a knee, for good measure pinion it with his hand, until the assemblage came undone and he began to slide out of his seat while furiously taking notes.

But the others were upset, too. Nor was Donato oblivious to their horror.

"*Bisognasse, vedi,*" he assured us: *They had to, you see.*

For Jack, it was the Slaughter of the Innocents come to life! He suggested as much to Donato, who irritably replied that these particular children were mostly bastard by-blows from the orphanage and hence technically no innocents, not in the Church of Rome sense of the word. He was moving on, when Michael's body untangled and his hand shot up.

"*Michele?*" Donato said.

But before Michael uttered a word—though he kept his left arm high—he finished some noisy thought on paper. This, I reflected, was what Michael could *do:* attack paper. According to Jack, what he couldn't do—sad for a would-be architect—was create anything. The attempt always balked and stymied him. This inability (doubtless a trauma resulting from his year of *doing* in Viet Nam) had caused him to tag along after Katie rather than waste time in an Adams U. design studio, but it also kept the fires of frustration going—fed those underground lodes of anger that squirted irregularly to the surface.

"*Professore!*" he erupted. "*Questa storia non mi posso credere!*

How could anyone send *kids* to certain death? That's *evil!*"

His Italian was still crude enough that Donato could affably pretend not to comprehend and begin talking about the construction of the *Fortezza Medicea*.

Michael interrupted.

"*Cattivo! Cattivissimo!* And you pretend it doesn't matter, that time makes up for everything? I mean, *we* have Viet Nam, but millions are marching—"

At mention of Viet Nam, Donato gave the *"Ahh!"* of a man served a savory, irresistible, altogether delectable dish. Sitting back as though a nice chat about Viet Nam were all he could desire, he practically loosened his belt as he started in on an elegant condemnation of America's Southeast Asia murder spree. With rhetorical skill, he reviewed the U.S.-sponsored assassination of President Diem and the build-up of American armies that proceeded to shoot, bomb and burn men, women, *children,* wittily centering more and more on Michael as the prototypical grunt who disclaimed responsibility even while pulling the trigger at atrocities like My Lai.

It would have been cruel had it not been, in essence, true.

Michael meanwhile shut up, looking at no one and nothing but regarding instead some terrible inner landscape. Briana put a hand on his arm and he shook it off. Jack leaned over to murmur something, but Michael jerked away. Katie intervened, putting her hand on Michael's and speaking into his ear. He closed his eyes and shuddered. I was glad he didn't have an M-16 to hand.

Stepping down beside Donato's desk, I interrupted his loving dissection of America's failing "Vietnamization" strategy.

"Basically you're talking about the same thing," I offered, throwing the Hail Mary pass of the teaching profession. "Truth is, Viet Nam's—"

"Fuck *you* know about truth?" snarled Michael with such force I absolutely took a step backwards into the wall.

"My intentions are good, I assure you," I told him.

"Give yourself a gold star, *professore*," he mocked. "How Americans believe in good intentions! They gild the vaults of heaven! No need seeing how they work out on the ground."

Donato beamed at his apt pupil while Katie whispered and Michael picked up their books and stood up. But before they went, he let us know one last thing.

"Where'd they plant LBJ, by the Perdenales? Won't be long before my buddies and me dig him up and drive a friggin' wooden stake through his heart. *Hey, hey, LBJ!*"

Katie put her long fingers to the back of his neck.

"Smile, Michael!" she commanded.

After a moment's resistance, he did so. It was grotesque. She pushed him firmly up the aisle and out the door. I signaled the class to stay quiet until they'd left the building. A mind is a terrible thing to waste, I reflected — waste being the *mot juste*.

Donato returned to the 16th century until the noontime peal of bells.

At siesta, the expulsion of the *bocche inutili* was all Jack could talk about. How he condemned those ancient Sienese!

Students enjoy the luxury of moral purity. I don't have much patience with it.

"Sometimes you just have to lighten the lifeboats, Jack," I said. "Give Donato credit for not covering up. They don't boast about it, you know. Though I bet they did at the time, it has such a *'Look what you made us do!'* quality."

He turned the big liquid eyes of stricken youth on me — the eyes, it struck me (and how Seventies the image!), of a space alien unfamiliar with Earthly usage. Earthly usage tends to narrow the eyes. Two tears came loose, pendant diamonds that left snail scum down his cheeks.

"Wipe your eyes, my *David*," I said, "and turn over."

"I hate your doing that, Gary, and you do it all the time," he snapped. "I'm not sculpture. I don't want to remind you of anyone or anything except myself. You see the world through an art-history filter—don't see *countryside*, but classic landscapes. You don't see *people*, you see statues or portraits."

"Mostly background figures," I joked. "Very acute, Jack. Perhaps I do look at the present through a window to the past, as it were, but—"

"A *closed* window that gives back your own reflection. More a *mirror*, in fact. As it were."

Had my work cut out to get what I wanted that afternoon.

12.

TOWARDS THE END of March the group, plus Prof. Donato and myself, hopped aboard a charter coach and sped down to Rome on a four-day field trip. We stayed at an ancient pilgrim monastery in the *Campagna*, that soulless waste which from ancient times has been the Roman greenbelt. There I had a room—cell, really—to myself, as did Prof. Donato. The others shared cells.

Never was I so full of farcical plots for sneaking someone into my bed. After a fatiguing day of sightseeing and dinner in the refectory, I would yawn and stretch, proclaim I was turning in early. A few minutes later Jack would repeat my performance, tap on my door and we would enjoy a soundless tryst in a tiny room probably consecrated to same-sex love for a thousand years, before he snuck off to sleep in the cell he shared with Michael. It was fun. (Meanwhile Michael illicitly snuck into Katie's and Briana's cell to massage poor Katie's back.)

But on our last full day—after a strenuous morning following Donato's upheld guidebook through the Vatican Museum's endless galleries and a group lunch at which he retailed the prevailing Italian theory that Watergate was a coup dreamed up by the CIA—we had a free afternoon, and Jack and I shook everybody. He had to feign temper in telling his friends he preferred to be alone, but alone we found ourselves. Rendezvousing on the Via Veneto, we wandered along, window-shopping and people-watching, then sat down at a café beside that classic tourist spot, the Trevi Fountain, and ordered *limonette*.

Big mistake.

Suddenly Jack looked serious.

I vividly remember the scene: the muffled crash of waters, with the occasional kiss of spray; scooters shooting past; high-revving cars in combat; the taste of my *limonetta*; even the nearby carillon (the strife of bells can drill a wormhole through time). Also Jack's beautiful earnest face, eyes narrowed against the sun but sunglasses conscientiously removed to assist his expression of sincerity as he told me how much I was coming to mean to him. If I were a painter (alas, a college course or two served to disabuse me), I would render a photorealist shot of that striking face. I kept asking myself, "What am I *doing* here?"

Remember, not only was Jack promiscuous (though I'm sure the word would have made him squirm), it was 1974:

Guys going at it hot and heavy simply didn't fall in love.

Jack never said *love*, but he told me how wonderful we were together.

"Don't tell me it's *over*?" I teased.

He declared he wanted to escape the miasma of Watergate-era America by staying in Italy and doing art history at the university in Florence, and I could doubtless get a job there, and together we could make a life.

"Young people love to make life decisions," I remarked — too lightly, judging from the way his face fell, but I wanted to keep things light. "*I* can't stay, and *you* might care to sleep on it, Jack. Bear in mind it's a good time to be getting back to the USA."

"What do you mean?" asked the innocent.

"I mean that all the energy that's been wasted on the Revolution and love and peace will soon be brought to bear on real things, and you don't want to get left behind. Meanwhile, until June we have a nice thing going, don't we?"

I gave him my sincerest smile. He was supposed to say I was right.

Instead, he looked like I'd punched him. He pondered aggrievedly at some deep level that left him no powers of speech, meanwhile reaching out and rubbing my thigh. Since we were sitting down, sweaters tied at our waists in what was then exclusively the European manner, and I thought a minute's rubbing would help him accept my terms on continuing our affair on a no-strings basis until the time came to let it die, I let him.

"Hi, guys!" pealed an American voice.

I forget her name, though I remember the group's nickname for her: *Bowling Ball*. She was a fat girl whose lack of physical blessings was complete. She was not a fat girl with a pretty face, a lovely voice and a sparkling personality, but a sodden drab with a skin condition, a foghorn and an utter lack of grace. For her to get up from table was to knock over her chair. For her to close a door was to slam it accidentally so hard people came running to see if it was another bomb from the Red Brigades. A nice girl and a good student, but so preoccupied with standing apart from a physical self that repelled her more than anybody that it left her a phenomenon: an American girl in Italy *senza* Italian suitors.

"What a coincidence!" she exclaimed, plopping herself down (spilling our drinks) and changing the film in her camera while exclaiming upon the odds against coming across us.

She was not an unperceptive person and, victim of people's talk though she was, a notorious gossip.

It made it worse that Jack, though he stopped rubbing my thigh, hadn't the wit to lift his hand, but remained limp and flowerlike inclining towards me. I lifted his hand off, myself. And believe me, Bowling Ball missed nothing.

"See those Germans?" she said, winding her film. "With the dyed hair? Think they're fags?"

"Who knows or cares?" I snapped.

"So what're you two up to this afternoon?" she asked. "Can I come along?"

It was very embarrassing. Jack had drawn an entirely unnecessary picture for her.

Excusing myself, I taxied back to our lodging, while Jack (a soft touch in every way) went off to tour *Castel Sant'Angelo* with his new girlfriend.

That phrase *in the closet* he threw at me in whispers that evening irked me then as it does now. I never lived in the closet, never set up housekeeping amidst raincoats and galoshes; no more than he! I simply had the dignity and self-respect to live my life discreetly. How I lived it was my business; no need to let the world in on it.

Jack and I were only eight years apart, but he was of a younger generation for all that—Woodstock Generation, though by now the kids are probably mixing up Woodstock with Watergate.

"I never said I wanted an exclusive thing with you, Jack," I whispered beneath the crude *Assumption of the Virgin* frescoed over my bed. "But you went ahead and signed me up for it anyway."

"You want to see other guys?" he said, pretending not to be shocked. "Go ahead. Let's *both* see other people."

"Lower your voice," I hissed. "Remember, I'm your teacher. Most people would say I'm not supposed to be fucking you."

"I'm not one of them," he said, "but if you're ashamed of me—"

"I just don't want you to think we're in a relationship when we're *not*. It's unfortunate you make me put it so bluntly, but let me remind you, no strings means *no strings*."

He drew himself up and said, "I don't think I want to be with you any more, Gary."

"Well, if that's how you feel," I said.

Graciousness was the order of the day; I knew hormones would deliver him to my siesta again. Opening the door to my cell, I looked to see that the coast was clear and nodded him out.

As I closed it I heard Bowling Ball say, "Why, *hello*, Jack."

But so far as I know she never said a word to anybody. Guess she wanted to keep up that grade point average.

13.

TO MY SURPRISE, Jack and I had no make-up tryst. We did not make up. He was scrupulous to engage in nothing personal with me. On Wednesdays it was funny to see him choose my parlor's stiffest chair, sit excruciatingly erect while discussing his bloody pictures. Of course I was distant with him, too.

He plugged away at his *Slaughters*, brought me Cercigano's, Rubens', Massolina's, a sepia print of Pisano's sculpture in Siena's own *Battistero*. After our disagreement in Rome his interest in them only deepened.

Easter vacation arrived in mid-April. Jack made plans with Briana, Katie and Michael to hitchhike to Naples and ferry across to Sicily, the island the Italian boot so stylishly kicks. This I learned from Briana; Jack shared nothing.

Accordingly, on the chosen morning, the quartet set off, walking out through *Porta Romana* into a countryside bursting into the *mille fiori* background of medieval tapestry. Even the pines and cypresses were reclaiming a more robust coloring as the spring sun leaped higher in the sky.

As they began fishing the road for rides Briana showed a new assertiveness. Rather than sinking herself within Jack's outline as before, she stepped away and confidently engaged the passing drivers.

"Katie and I talked about it," she giggled. "This is *Italy*, Jack. Drivers want a *woman*. You and Michael are just along for the ride."

The commodity value Italians put on her as a female was, for a strait-laced Midwesterner, new and unnerving; but then again, what but instinct brought her to Italy? *L'Autostop* was helping to liberate that instinct. One northward jaunt had put them in a Peugeot piercing tunnel after tunnel through the Apennines towards Bologna. Every time darkness enveloped them the driver placed his hand on Briana's knee. He must have thought she was stone, she remained so rigid, however insinuatingly he caressed tendon or bone. But inside, something was beginning to stir.

This day Jack and Briana were being set down at a tollbooth of the *Autostrada del Sole* near Chiusi, on their intended direct route to Naples, when the driver mentioned he was continuing on to Spoleto, and suddenly the prospect of waiting where *carabinieri* might shoo them away seemed charmless next to the idea of improvising a route through the Abruzzi and Campania.

At dusk their serpentine track through the hills had brought them past Spoleto to L'Aquila. They found a *pensione* in that remote, impoverished town, ate and settled in early. In the national gloom enforced by 15-watt reading lamps, Jack read *Paese Sera* (a Communist paper with headlines printed in red) and the latest *Topolino,* the comic book he found a treasure house of idioms. He didn't intend to ignore Briana, but that she felt snubbed dawned on him as she conducted a noisy if subtle protest.

Women do this. The hostile (because silent) act of reading can provoke them into making a racket. Male concentration and the deafness and blindness it entails, the lag in response women encounter when they seek verbal reassurance (as they do every few minutes) infuriates them.

With mighty whines Briana unzipped compartments of her pack and slapped down objects, snapped caps on pens, pulled tops off bottles, set to wiping surfaces with wadded-up tissues. Then she took off her jeans and shirt (relying as ever on Jack's innate gentlemanliness not to peek), climbed into bed, threw out her locks and combed and combed and brushed and brushed. This had a self-soothing aspect, but also one of attack.

Jack found he couldn't follow his comic book. Surrendering, he put it aside and, as he lounged unselfconsciously in his skivvies, they began to chat. His body was more innocent of muscular cladding than young men's bodies nowadays, but sitting against the pillows would have defined a washboard in his skinny belly. As Briana brushed they spoke with the sweet breath of babies.

Though he may have been unable to catch the signals of invitation sparking off her, he fell asleep convinced she was taking more of the covers than usual, and woke up the next morning possibly less clueless than before.

They continued down Italy's spine, discovering hill towns of a more rugged stamp than Tuscany's. All that next day their eyes tended to meet in a new way.

That evening they fetched up in Benevento. They dined, strolled across the Roman *Ponte Leproso*, returned to the youth hostel and on the landing of the women's dormitory wished each other good night. The men's dorm of pushed-together bunkbeds was mostly filled by an Austrian college group. In the middle of the night Jack woke up in the embrace of the boy on the next bunk. Whose volition did that embrace embody? Who grabbed first? Both blinked and disengaged and went back to sleep.

Next day they reached Naples. After getting a hotel room, they went out to see the town. Its liveliness made their eyes gleam; even a patdown on the street by child beggars amused them. In a dusty park Briana announced she wanted to see Jack hanging upside down, so obligingly he climbed a tree and swung by his knees from a bough. She laughed and laughed.

At Pompeii they visited the famous brothel, whose frescoes show bronze-skinned males fucking cream-colored females in every possible way. The dirtiest images were covered by cloths, which leering guards pulled aside in exchange for a 500*l* note. Outdoors they came upon a cloth covering part of a wall; Jack lifted it to find a fresco of a flagrant erection. When they saw an entire sheet ahead, Briana ran up giggling and whipped it away, revealing a chaste still life of fruits and flowers.

Back in Naples, they met up with Michael and Katie outside the *Museo Nazionale*. The four stayed up late drinking wine.

Next day they booked an overnight voyage to Sicily. I know that wild island a little, and can vouch for how visiting it feels like stepping off the edge of the Earth. During my junior year abroad (in Florence), I journeyed to Taormina in search of documentary evidence concerning Baron von Gloeden, friend of Wilde's (and one wonders who else). Von Gloeden photographed generations of scrawny peasant lads, posing them nude in cornball classical settings that highlighted their genitalia—cocks flung from the fist of God Himself!—and conducted a lively mail-order business with the prints. (In the event, I didn't get far, but that's another story.)

Just at sunrise Palermo pulled itself over a taut sea to them. It was too early when they landed to get rooms, so they stumbled from the harbor through blocks bombed-out in World War II to a park where they napped on the grass. A lion's roar finally woke them up; it came from the adjoining zoo. Then with the renewable energy of kids they hiked out to what Katie, especially, was wild to see: the Capuchin catacombs. On view there, as guidebooks blithely inform you, are 8,000 naturally mummified corpses—centuries' worth of the cream of Palermo society.

Curious, at my age I've exhausted any interest in the dead human body, but I vaguely remember that for the young it's different, that death and decay have an allure. They found the church annex that housed the entrance, paid admission to an impassive friar and walked downstairs to a cool tunnel network extending hundreds of yards.

Briana gripped Jack's arm, Katie grabbed Michael's, they went in two directions. Bare bulbs dangled at intervals and grit dusted everything. On the walls two rows of corpses hung suspended by the shoulders. Gravity pulled the faces clear of expression. Eyelids askew hinted at vacancies within. Death pried open the mouths and made them scream. Burial finery was rotting to reveal withered and eaten-away flesh. Where there was room between heads, babies filled the gap. One stood togaed like a Roman senator, infant elbow thoughtfully crooked on a pillar to support a featureless face: *memento mori*. Iron bars closed off a ghoulish workspace where spare limbs lay about. Nothing—no glass or rope—intervened between the kids and the *defunti* as they progressed at a museum two-step amidst this cascade, this spilling wealth of cadavers.

Jack and Briana crept along until they came to a particular eyeless corpse in frockcoat and top hat whose lips someone had accessorized with a cigarette. Briana tugging Jack away, they hurried upstairs, past the now grinning friar, and in the fresh air burst out laughing—somewhat hysterically.

Michael and Katie already sat in the shade of a wall, near a splash of blood in the street. Michael, shaken, for once paler than Katie (who in fact had color in her cheeks and light in her eyes), told them what happened: They no sooner sat down than a distinctly unwell pigeon wobbled past. Michael reached to scoop it up and comfort it, but to escape him it made a beeline into the street, where a Fiat flattened it.

Michael looked so beseechingly at Jack the skin on his arms prickled.

"Guys mind if we push on? Today? Place creeps me out."

14.

BEFORE THE SUN had quite set, their train arrived at the place once known as *Girgenti*, now more euphoniously, if less mysteriously, *Agrigento*, a town on the south coast founded by the Greeks. All afternoon the engine had pulled them through hills bright with flowers past flocks of sheep feeding near crouching shepherds. They shared a compartment with a magnificent old man six-and-a-half feet tall whose blue eyes flashed northern blood 900 years after the Norman conquest of Sicily. He skinned blood oranges for them with flicks of his knife. Michael said hardly a word the whole trip.

They took rooms at a hotel near the station and hurried down to the promontory over the sea where stood the Greek temples. Approaching them, they passed Pirandello's boyhood home (to note which, it strikes me, is Pirandellian). The sunset red that had drenched the countryside was seeping away, leaving a textured darkness scented by pines.

From a long marble terrace rose three temples, most of whose columns still raked the skyline, some even supporting roof elements. The drums of other columns had rolled partway down the hill. The four felt something uncanny, possibly the presence of the ancient gods in this elemental world of cylinders, straight lines, stone, sea and sky. Dangling their legs over the terrace's edge, they watched the western sky recall its last spears of light from the fading pageant. Michael and Katie murmured privately. Rust and gold flecked Briana's calm eyes as she sat, fingers wedged in her armpits against the splendor of the view. Jack felt alive to something new in her released by some sanction or blessing in the air. He scrutinized her face and felt rewarded when she looked at him.

When darkness had expunged the scene they returned to the hotel. After dinner, Michael and Katie bade their friends goodnight. Briana showered, then sat up in bed brushing her hair. Jack took a shower also. As warm water sluiced over his body he meditated on the Greeks and their pan-sexuality, on me and my supposed heartlessness, on his own dictatorial horniness. A towel wrapped around his waist, he solemnly got into bed and damply regarded Briana.

"*What?*" she demanded.

"Nothing."

She continued to brush, he to watch her. A minute later he reached out, and she put down her hairbrush and let him hold her.

They adjusted their positions and he kissed her, gently plumbing her mouth.

What followed seemed the most natural thing in the world. He wasn't used to worrying about birth control, but she whispered that she was on the Pill. There was a little blood, but Jack was fazed neither by it nor by the cry of pain she couldn't suppress.

"It's my first time, too," he confided. (It never occurred to him what a whopper he was telling.)

He felt rather detached throughout the act, especially at his orgasm, when he came in the same way I did with him once, pushing along, keeping himself at the brink, then tidily climaxing at his own convenience, nothing mutual about it. When *I* did this, he blazed up with resentment, but Briana didn't appear to mind.

Everything was pleasant until, as she fell asleep, she murmured, "I love you, Jack."

That did it for him. He withdrew from her tangle of arms and legs and fretted in a very young man's long night of the soul. It occurred to him that he was in love, too—with *me*. Guilt assailed him! He'd done a terrible thing! Parted her legs and put it in! And gotten off on it! When he loved Another!

But however bad he felt, he also felt good: He'd taken the triumphal march that makes a man a man. If he had no special interest in doing it again, at least he'd done it. And been on top to boot, as he never was with me (never).

He decided to forgive my behavior in Rome, and to tell me so at our next meeting. Decision made, he slept the sleep of a baby.

If Jack was deficient in tenderness towards Briana, he was full of it for himself. But he was, after all, in love.

At dawn's ghostly light Briana rolled into him and said, "*Ouch!*" And he ignored her, save to urge her out of bed to catch sunrise at the temples. He not only made no move for her, he pretended nothing had happened between them. Off he went, knocking up Michael and Katie, and returning to chivy Briana: Hurry, the sun was coming up!

Briana was a stoic American girl, one of millions who survived an era when no one, not even themselves, valued their virginity. Having found a way to be disburdened of it in a sincere manner that wouldn't lead to pregnancy, she knew she had no cause for complaint.

They duly trudged back to the temples to watch the sunrise. Sun scoured their faces and seemed to blur the columns' ancient fluting. Morning lacked evening's subtlety; the gods had fled. A path lured them down to the dark shore, where chilly mist clung to the beach. Near by, boats were pulled up and fishermen repairing their nets. Katie wandered off collecting shells. Up above, the colonnades bristled with sunlight. But eventually sun reached down to the shore and began to dissolve the mist and warm the sand. As though the gods had stolen back, intent on playful interference with mortals, Katie sank beneath a sky stretched with cheesecloth and fell asleep. The others watched over her from a concrete escarpment.

Soon they noticed a *tizio* their age walking over from the boats, curious about Katie. Jack told me he never saw a more beautiful male than this youth in jeans and fisherman's blouse, with his tight black curls, luminous dark eyes, narrow hips. The young man stole near Katie, stopped and studied her, then, crouching, feigning interest in the sand, stole nearer still.

"Should we—?" asked Jack.

Michael said, "No."

The young man's approach resembled that of the faun in Debussy's *Prelude*—belonging more to myth than to life. For ten minutes he circled the sleeping beauty. He soon gave up the pretense of searching the sand, but would squat and regard her for a minute, then circle her, crouching again a few paces closer. She was oblivious. Once, shifting her position, she froze him mid-step. Michael bore the saddest face Jack ever saw.

Finally the young man settled on his haunches beside Katie's head and reached to pet it. They could see the play of wonder on his face. After a minute of his gentle stroking she awakened and angled herself up on her arms, blinking. He spoke, doubtless in the incomprehensible local dialect, gesturing at the sea and the boats. Her face was alive, blushing, bore a succession of expressions not seen before. Smoothing her hair, she said something. The breeze took most of it, but Jack heard, "*non capisco*... I don't understand..."

Michael eased himself off the concrete and shambled over, Jack and Briana following. Jack even shook the breathtaking young man's hand. The youth had eyes only for Katie. She was hugging herself for warmth and complaining that she couldn't understand him. Michael tentatively put an arm around her.

The young man retrieved a pink shell from his pocket, offered it and began to recede, woe stretched across his face. Not unlike Debussy's fable, the scene dissolved bittersweet, unresolved.

"He was so *beautiful*," Katie said as they trudged up the slope to town.

15.

MICHAEL ANNOUNCED THAT he and Katie were cutting short their trip and returning to Siena by train.

Jack and Briana saw them off before lunch. As the train was sliding away Briana leaned her weight against him, and Jack realized that he'd neither outwaited nor otherwise solved his false position.

They spent one more night in Agrigento, a perfectly chaste one. Neither made a move. Neither said a word.

Next morning they set out on the road for Messina, immediately catching a long ride from a sad man in the meat trade. At 11:00 o'clock they were beached in the interior of Sicily on a hillside within view of oxen plowing. More farm carts than cars passed, and most of those cars tooted their horns and sped onwards. Those drivers who slowed at sight of them launched streams of dialect, once or twice garnished with gestures about the chin. That was slightly scary.

By noon they'd hiked to an almost deserted stone village,

where the only people stirring were old women blanketed in black. Breaking out the *panini* and mineral water they brought from Agrigento, they sat in a crumb of shade in the *piazza* to eat.

Water gushing from a marble lion's head, Briana suggested they give up trying to hitchhike and take the train instead, spending the time thus saved in Sorrento or even Capri. Jack protested that he wanted to hitchhike at least to Siracusa, that she had agreed to that plan. She extrapolated their morning's difficulty forward. He held out for the serendipitous revelations of hitchhiking. She said the Sicilian countryside scared her.

Jack reacted as though she'd questioned his masculinity. No female timidity was going to spoil *his* trip!

"Do what you want, Briana," he snapped. "See you in Siena." He hoisted his pack and stalked away.

"Jack," she called, "don't do this."

He walked out of sight. She had a choice of chasing him down with apologies or of getting to a train station as fast as she could and heading north.

Of course she did the latter. A sweet woman in a Jaguar gave her a ride, with the result that in ten minutes Briana was at the nearest station, and in 15, by fortunate happenstance, aboard an express for the mainland.

Jack chased his own rage for two miles. He didn't even put out his thumb, but walked as though walking kept his actions retrievable. Then, his rage gone, he came to himself on a red-earth roadside, harrowed with fear at what might, because of him, be happening to Briana.

He crossed the road. He must have looked just like the *David* as he hooked that thumb. Soon he was in a car going back the way he came. Its driver kindly helped him make inquiries and they learned of Briana's ride. At the station, they found that she'd boarded a train. Jack felt better.

In token of repentance, he gave up his tour of Sicily and waited (and waited) for the next train.

16.

EARLY THE FOLLOWING EVENING Michael and I dined on *calzoni* outside Bar Costa. He was heavy going, but the *Mensa* was closed for Easter and I couldn't very well tell him I preferred to eat by myself. Besides, he'd turned up in Siena with a particularly gloomy air; I sensed something had occurred to impair his linkage with Katie, who was back at her *pensione*. Anyway, my *calzone* was delicious—goat cheese steaming beneath folds of *prosciutto* and shards of egg. Chianti complemented it perfectly.

Eating and drinking, we absorbed and tested the *Campo*'s quality. As people entered, greetings rang across. Michael had just remarked that the *Campo* owed part of its charm to the fact that it wasn't too large for anyone not to recognize an acquaintance across it, and I had to admit he'd hit the nail on the head. The vastness of the *Piazza San Marco*, for instance, makes everyone a stranger, but the only strangers in the *Piazza del Campo* are people you don't know.

The light was the flattering last light of day, a general rejuvenating blush, except where one bright ray still cut through from the Banchi di Sopra. Night began to pull a curtain across the *Campo*'s glowing complex curves. After taking Roman sunbaths all day — stretches in the sun, followed by plunges into shade — the cats came alive and began to roam. Meanwhile the splashing of the *Fonte Gaia* absorbed the sounds of footfalls and conversation.

Half a dozen of Siena's own gay guys sat a few tables off, daring half-stifled rudenesses about people passing. Because they tended to congregate at this same Bar Costa, I had a nodding acquaintance with them. Half of them were pretty, half hideous.

Another of them was making his customary orbit of the *Campo* as if it were the ninth circle of hell, a hatchet-faced man with, I judged, at least one sock stuffed into his crotch. He would lean on a stanchion and look around, give Michael and me sharp glances. Then he would move on, peering into every face, his acute profile ready to swing backwards in a trice. He was as watchful as the pigeons who flew crazy sky patterns before dropping beside our table to peck at crumbs; watchful as the cats who padded stealthily after the pigeons.

A person stepped into the *Campo* at its farthest reach — a handsome figure in a dress, though I was sure no one I knew. I looked brazenly at that face and body, surprised by my thought: "I wish that were Briana and we could sit in this beautiful dusk, drink wine, talk of serious things, and later go home together."

Then I thought, "It does *look* like Briana, but it *can't* be, she's in the South with that what's-his-name who begins to bore me, instead it's some awful stranger."

Then the sun's last diagonal disrobed her — dissolved that dress and left her nude. And the *Campo*'s clamshell closed on my heart and brought me to my feet, for it *was* Briana.

"*Briana!*"

She looked over. The furrow in her brow filled and she

smiled.

"*Professore! Michele!*"

As she came up I could see in her eyes that she knew exactly what she wanted.

"Call me Gary," I said. "But when did you get back? How was Sicily? Where's Jack? Why the dress?"

She smiled.

"Because I want to eat a good meal at a restaurant like a grown-up, Gary."

"Will the Costa do? Sit down, join us. You look wonderful."

She ate a *calzone* with good appetite while telling us about Jack's abandoning her. That surprised and angered us. Fortunate for him that she'd returned safely. About their sexual passage she said nothing, but I possess certain intuitive powers of discernment (which Jack later ungallantly confirmed).

After Michael left us, I suggested over espresso that she come look at my new coffee-table book on Masaccio. Stiffening in her seat, she tightened her grip on the purse in her lap like a rider taking up the reins.

"All right, Gary. Sure."

Masaccio served to bring our thighs together. Over a reproduction of *Sant'Anna Metterza* I put my lips to hers. She responded, but I pressed her no further that evening.

Late the next afternoon, as Briana was freshening up after a pre-prandial apéritif of Cynar and soda, there came a knock at my door.

I opened it to the picture of misery: Jack. He came in familiarly, uninvited, but looking so beaten down I had no heart to stop him.

"Gary, have you seen Briana? Has *anyone* seen her?"

"I thought she was with you," I said.

"Oh God, what a mess," he said. "And it's all my fault."
Briana walked in.
"Hello, Jack."
"Briana!" His voice was strangled with joy.
"Shall we go?" she asked me.

His gladness gave way to horror, though his apologies flowed until Briana's brusque forgiveness cut him short.

We did not invite him to join us. At the bottom of the steps we turned towards the *Campo*. Looking back, I found Jack still watching us with horror.

17.

ONE EVENING EARLY in May, Jack, Michael and Katie decided to make the 7:00 o'clock showing of *Gimme Shelter*, the Maysles brothers' documentary about the Altamont music festival, only four years in reaching *Cinema Luna* (Briana had a dinner date with me). Having seen it in the States, Michael pronounced it the essential film of our time. As they walked from the *Mensa* to Piazza Matteotti, he regaled girlfriend and roommate with his insights.

"Altamont was our generation's Nuremberg rally," he told them. "*You'll* see. The Hells Angels guarding the stage are stoned and drunk and out for trouble. The Stones start playing *Sympathy for the Devil*, and the crowd goes *crazy*. Fights break out. Mick halts the music, tells his mates, 'I'll try and stop it.'

To the crowd he muses in his flattered celebrity way, 'Something very funny always happens when we start that number.' He minces around pretending it's about them not paying attention, when really it's about *him* energizing chaos and death. They start playing again, but someone knocks over a motorcycle, and Angels go nuts. You see a flashing arc. That's the knife going in. Keith Richards crosses himself, and keeps playing."

As a bus came along, filling the width of the street, they stepped into a doorway with the practiced ease of the Sienese.

"Mick will have none of it," Michael resumed. "Mick has *had* it! 'We don't want to fight,' he says, and tells the Angels, 'Hey! We're *splitting!*' But he means it like a child would, even improvises a child's lyric: '*Bye-bye-bye, Bye-bye-bye.*'

"Adolf Jagger's a rock god—which is a god that can't do a friggin' thing except excite people. Our generation's marching—I don't know where. But bad shit's coming."

As usual, they bought candy at Bar Lantini before the show so they could ignore the sad-sack usher who roamed the aisles with stale candy on a tray. Katie stayed outside to inspect the fashion magazines hanging from the newsstand.

Bar Lantini sold its sugar-coated chocolates by weight through Lucite chutes that permitted one to select different colors. Michael judiciously turned spigots for Katie's favorite greens, yellows and reds, while avoiding her anathema blues.

As candies poured down Katie was in the corner of Jack's eye, one hand clutching the ends of her hair, as absent-minded or intent as Michael himself. As frequently happened, a man with a camera came up to her. She was always happy to pose. Jack turned to watch as the man, looking through the viewfinder, directed her a little to the side where the pavement was neither distinctly roadway nor walkway. Katie launched her biggest smile and a Topolino darted into her and sent her flying up like a rag doll. She came down on her head.

People ran over. Jack grabbed Michael, but he was waiting with his waxed-paper sack for his change, so initially resisted.

When they got there and frantically penetrated the crowd, Katie was lying face up against a spreading aureole of blood, her eyes open but glazed and empty. The photographer knelt in blood calling, *"Bella, Bella."* Candies splashed in the puddle as Michael jammed his face to hers.

Things happened in their inevitable course. *Polizia* showed up, an ambulance arrived, medics attended to Katie before hoisting her into the rear. Michael scrambled up to accompany her, and they wailed down Via di Città to the *Ospedale Santa Maria della Scala*, scattering the last of the *passeggiatta.*

The police questioned the Fiat's driver, but it was an accident of the sort accepted wherever there are cars: He hadn't *meant* to plow into a person, so bore no fault for having done so.

When Jack got to the *Ospedale* Katie was hooked up to machines that made a rhythmic racket as though voicing complaints from beyond the veil. Michael sat in a corner, his pale face outlined in red. To Jack the doctors denied the self-evident fact that Katie was dead. The nurses, promising to pray in shifts overnight, firmly shoved him and Michael out into the *Piazza del Duomo*. Jack had fits of crying after they got home; dealing with them gave Michael something to do. Michael was cool about the whole thing.

The hospital's early morning call waking me up, I got there shortly after a priest performed last rites and the machines were unplugged, in time to see them pull a sheet over Katie's face. Her features were so white, so perfect they might have been carved from Carrara marble by Jacopo della Quercia.

I called her family (as Michael had not). With the satellite delay we talked over each other until comprehension dawned in screams across the Atlantic. Getting the body coffined and crated, taken to Fiumicino Airport and placed aboard a plane took an inordinate number of forms on official stamped paper to accomplish.

Probably Michael's indifference to the mere clay was a battlefield lesson. Declining to accompany the body home, he acquired a bag of hashish and secreted himself.

The group was devastated, of course, Briana especially so, and Katie's *Mensa* admirers were bereft. We conducted a kind of memorial service, scandalizing the *Università* by doing so neither in its chapel nor in the sandy cemetery outside the walls, where enameled oval photographs adorn the markers, but in the garden beside our classroom building. Tears were shed, stories offered, roses tossed to her photograph and furled umbrella. Everybody waxed dutifully fatalistic—"her time" and so forth, in our poverty-stricken modern formulations.

Jack felt very sorry for himself. A semester of suffering! Learning about the *cacciata delle bocche inutili* left him raw; my extreme cruelty, not to mention my interest in Briana, rubbed salt in the wound. Now this too-close experience of death's instantaneous finality chased him out of town. Hoisting his pack, he walked out through *Porta Fontebranda*. Its arch opens to a downhill slope where ancient springs bubble and mean cats meow invective. He took up his stance, raised his thumb and was gone a week.

18.

ONE WARM EVENING ten or twelve days later Briana and I were dining outside Bar Costa. Being open about my interest in her did neither of us any harm. After all, a man nearing 30 had better look interested in getting married—or something like it—or people will assume he's gay.

As we ate Jack and Michael cut through the *Campo* on their way home from the *Mensa*. Michael entered with what I took to be jungle reconnaissance technique, both hands on the wall as he put one foot in front of the other, then pivoted his body. Probably he was playing, but it gave me the creeps.

"*Don't look this way,*" I implored *sotto voce*. "*Don't look this way.*"

But Briana waved at them. Mercifully, Jack tapped his wrist where a watch would have been had he worn one and kept going, but Michael came over with the eagerness of an old setter dog, sat down and ordered *birra*.

I never liked to encourage his nutty monologues, but he was our poster boy for grief, after all. And this evening he seemed lucid.

"*Professore*, had a brainstorm about why the *Campo*'s shaped like a clamshell and/or the palm of a hand. It's because the pilgrim road crosses it, coming *di qua*"—he pointed towards *Porta Camollia*, then towards *Porta Romana*—"and going *di là*.

"Know *Romeo and Juliet?*" He slapped his palm to Briana's. "'For saints have hands that pilgrims' hands do touch/And palm to palm is holy palmer's kiss.' See, the wordplay works in both languages. In England they called pilgrims *palmers* because they brought home palm branches to show they got there, and in Italian they're *palmieri*. But hands have palms, too—*le mani hanno le palme.*"

"Wow," I said.

"Another pilgrim symbol? The clamshell. *Ecco tutto*. The *Campo*'s a representation of its function—it *embodies* what it is. They should pave it in mother of pearl!"

"That's really brilliant, Michael."

We lauded him until a one-eyed cat came creeping by and his mood plunged.

"Here kitty, kitty," he called. It ignored him but tensed at the sound of pigeon wings. We attended to our dinners. He was thinking, we knew, of Katie and her kindness towards these same creatures. "Look," he said, "the standing cat rocks forward with every breath." After a pause in which he seemed to pull himself together he asked, "Anyone seen Henry?"

A rumor had swept the town that Henry Kissinger was coming, that a Sixth Fleet helicopter would land him in the *Campo* for some sightseeing. And it was true he was in Italy: Footsteps of doom noisy in their ears, Nixon and his sinister Secretary of State were making a flurry of overseas trips to drum up some last roars of adulation.

"Not yet," I told Michael, and enjoyed myself pointing out the unlikelihood of landing a Sea Stallion in the *Campo*. I reminded him of another absurd rumor a few weeks earlier: that Pope Paul VI was strolling the streets. Certainly an old man in crimson—some Cardinal or other—had dispensed blessings outside the *Basilica di San Domenico* to a throng that included girls of our group who could not be persuaded that it wasn't the Pope they'd seen. No, no, someone had yelled *"Il papa!"* and that was good enough for them.

I was holding forth thus when a procession of chunky Alfa Romeo sedans flashing blue lights entered the *Campo* and swung into its middle. Now, cars go most places in Italy—at St. Peter's, you better watch out for the Mercedes limousines shooting through the piazza, scattering the faithful while whoever's in the backseat adjusts his skullcap—but they do *not* enter the *Piazza del Campo!*

Two black Cadillacs followed. Security men, obvious as hell—big guys in lumpy suits—gathered at one of them, and Henry Kissinger stepped out of it, a squat fleshy man, expressionless save that within his glasses glowed the thrill of the geek getting all the attention. An ample-breasted young woman and a nervous official of some kind joined him.

They goggled up at the *Palazzo del Comune* and *Torre del Mangia,* then revolved to admire the façades fronting the *Campo.* Their group reminded me of the animated little clusters Canaletto drops into his cityscapes. Then they disappeared into the *Palazzo,* probably for a look at Lorenzetti's fresco The Allegory of Good Government and Bad Government. I wondered what Henry would make of it.

Closer to us, that cat clapped two party hats on his head, pounced on a pigeon distracted by the motorcade and ran off with it fluttering in its mouth.

"Ever notice, a cat doesn't tell you he's going to do something?" Michael remarked. "Just does it."

Soon Henry and party emerged into the *Campo* again, apparently having found nothing in Lorenzetti to detain them. Some townspeople recognized him and in a small way mobbed him (then again, whatever their nominal nationalities, Nixon and Kissinger shared notably Italian temperaments).

While Henry signed autographs, Michael stood up and moved in his direction, not thinking to put down his bottle of beer.

Then he began to run.

It happened fast. Glass broke and Michael skidded on his head across the bricks. Whether he slipped on his own spilled beer or on spray thrown off by the *Fonte Gaia,* I don't know, but down he went with the exaggeration of a cartoon figure.

This happened many safe yards away from Henry, and his security detail was not unduly concerned—not even duly concerned. While we went up to Michael where he lay groaning, Henry peeped over as though thinking of dispatching a restorative autograph. Instead, he and his party got into their cars and were driven away.

Michael's nose was bleeding, his palms and cheek were skinned, pants knees torn. Mortified, he permitted me to walk him to a bus stop on Via di Città.

I rejoined Briana and, riveted by the moonrise, we lingered at Bar Costa. The moon rose seething and bloody, but its upward passage blanched it until it looked like a skull fragment circling the night.

Jack woke up before dawn to a variation of the usual scene: towels stuffed under the door, smoke heavy in the air, Michael nude. He was packing.

Jack asked what was up, and Michael sat down and spoke earnestly.

"It's a sign, man. When you can't even bop Henry one, it's a sign. I'm going to Persepolis like Katie dreamed of. Worked it out: Trieste, Dubrovnik, Athens, Istanbul, Persia. Then maybe East: Afghanistan. India. Kashmir." Inhaling, he said in the ghost of a voice, *"Kashmir,* brother man."

"Shouldn't you get some sleep first?"

Michael lay back and released a cloud of smoke. Jack fell asleep again and had a dream about Michael dissolving. When—at his landlady's *"Giacomo!"*—he woke up eager to report it, Michael was gone.

None of us saw him again. For Michael, life was the experience of pain through time, and I hope he made it East and found peace there.

19.

FINALS ARRIVED AT the end of May. They exacted their toll of angst, though no one had cause to worry. My art history test consisted of asking the class to identify slides and comment briefly. Everybody passed with flying colors. Donato administered his usual tough essay exam, but he'd long since learned to grade the *Springtime in Siena* group with a leniency his native students never knew.

But before classes officially ended, Briana and Jack presented us with the fruits of independent study.

Briana went first. She snapped through slides of a representative roster of the *Madonna col Bambino*, before showing us Duccio's *Maestà*, flooding the classroom with Mary's cerulean — nay, *celestial* — blue. When she forgot to step out of the way of the projector's beam she took her place in the picture as an attending angel. She argued for *Madonna col Bambino* as a kind of Oedipal scene, the infant representing baby *and* man, in both states protected by the female — a reversal of the cliché — and thus linked to the genre of the *Pietá*, the Madonna enfolding her dead adult son. I thought it a deep insight. Briana earned her applause and her A+++.

Alas, poor Jack apparently thought his was to be the final word on the semester — that it was up to him to sum up the group's experience of brutality and slaughter.

He read us St. Mathew's story of the three wise men following their star who share with King Herod their joy that the King of the Jews is born. The word *king* catching his attention, Herod suggests they drop by after they've located Him, but a dream warns them and they go home another way instead. Meanwhile Joseph's warning dream sends him with his family safe to Egypt.

> Then Herod, when he saw that he was mocked of the wise men, was exceeding wroth, and... slew all the children that were in Bethlehem, and in all the coasts thereof, from two years old and under.

Working crisply through slides of various *Slaughters of the Innocents*, Jack educated us in the genre's elements. His presentation was impeccable—until he veered off the track and projected Breughel the Elder's very different *Massacre of the Innocents*, a northern village scene (ca. 1565) of a genocidal episode illustrating not St. Mathew but the Hapsburg subjugation of Flanders.

Next he smashed Danieli di Volterra's picture on the wall. It glowed vivid, horrible, its cyclonic butchery leaping almost into the third dimension. As little mindful as Briana of avoiding the projector's light, Jack waded in blood, his pointer making him another swordsman as he ranged round the vortex, finding the pyramidal scenes of mothers, killers and infants punctuating it, and the center hub of piled-up baby corpses.

Jack likened the composition not only to electrons whirling about a nucleus (!), but to the shape of Omega, last word of the Greek alphabet, as though Daniele were suggesting the bloodshed represented some ultimate end point. He stood up there nobly performing an American youth's grand act of redemption by condemning everything in sight, including his own initial response.

"Its frenzy repelled me," he confessed. "I thought the Mannerist stylistics were part of Daniele's denial that kids were dying, but really his picture's frenzied *because* he's trying to express how *awful* it was, how *wrong*. Because only on the surface is his picture about King Herod. Remember Siena's expulsion of the *bocche inutili* in 1555? *That's* his real subject."

Inwardly I groaned.

"Florence sacked Daniele's native Volterra in 1530, when he was our age, so we can infer his feelings about Florence. And he actually studied right here in Siena. This picture he painted in Rome in 1556 or '57, just after Siena's siege, and details suggest Siena as the scene. See the open gate from which the action flows downhill? Very like the *Porta Fontebranda*. And could that be Siena's *Duomo* at the horizon? He's assimilating the *biblical* genre to Siena's *historical* event in order to *emphasize* the latter's horror.

"Which brings it full circle, because I doubt Siena would have *done* what it did without the *fact* of that genre. Follow?

"Remember, for centuries her citizens grew up surrounded by pretty pictures of babies being killed—quite a local specialty, in fact. During the siege someone must have noticed, say, a Mateo di Giovanni *Slaughter* and said, 'Hey, here's how to stretch our food, buy some time!' What they had hanging on their walls let them think the unthinkable and then *do* it—push kids and old people out the gates to be massacred."

I could stand it no longer.

"Please, Jack, sheathe your sword," I called. "Talking art history doesn't make you the artist manqué. Nothing's stopping *you* from painting the siege of Siena, but that happens not to be *this* picture's subject. I kind of like your 'Omega' point, but probably what Daniele's suggesting Herod's slaughter put the period to was the pre-Christian era."

"What the Sienese did was so horrible," Jack intoned, "it *can't* have gone unmemorialized in art."

"Except that it has," I said. "Daniele's inspired you to clever theorizing, but you know with me *clever* is seldom a term of praise. You're being judgmental—reading into this what you think *should* be there."

"Babies being put to the sword cries out for a little judgment."

"And attention must be paid!" I mocked. "Look, Daniele's putting his energetic Mannerist spin on an old tradition, not writing a newspaper story. It's an effective picture, but art is neither journalism nor history, Jack.

"I think you might be projecting onto Danieli something of *your* situation—that of a college student who's enjoyed a blissful springtime in Siena, but is now a semester closer to being on his own. Naturally you feel victimized—put to the sword by *life,* as it were, even if the draft *is* over!

"It's the old story of spoiled youth—sorry I can't think of a nicer word—upset to find out that growing up means, well, *growing up*. Welcome to the real world, Jack."

There were titters from the class.

"Look, people," I said, blood and gore washing over me as I stood up to face them. "The war's winding down, Watergate's building to a climax, soon we'll have a new President. This is a moment of pause before the next thing starts—the post-war *peace* thing—and I suggest that you of the Now Generation take a moment, drink a refreshing Pepsi and get down to the serious business of replicating your parents' lives as closely as you can.

"That's what it's about, after all, and always has been. Sure, it means contradicting your rhetoric, going from Revolution to B-school, macramé to marriage. It's a jump, but a jump everybody has to make sooner or later, because the world is what it is and there's no more good to be had from the Sixties love-and-peace bullshit."

And with that wild, inappropriate, unprofessional exhortation, I'd lost it. I was speaking as no teacher should.

Then again, they were practically my last words in a classroom. And Briana (bless her) was beaming support at me.

Oh well, Jack got his *A*. But where was Michael when I needed him? Probably he could have added well-observed points about slaughtered babies from personal experience.

20.

THAT VERY NIGHT I'm afraid I broke my vow not to bed Briana before the end of the semester made her no longer my student and thus fair game. But the moment arrived.

She came over for dinner, for my specialty, *spaghetti carbonara*. It went over well. We began kissing with the smoky flavor of *prosciutto* still in our mouths and continued with rich red wine. Eventually, I confessing I'd never been with a woman, she led me to the sheets.

But she was dizzier with Chianti than she knew. After pouring forth kindnesses, she threw her head back and went quiet. My murmurs and caresses went unanswered. As she lay clothed but with legs open and top unprotected, I began a stealthy and extremely exciting exploration. Unbuttoning her blouse, shifting her bra, I filled my eyes with a vision tastier than anything a man can offer. My lips teased hers while my hand played below. As I stroked her panties her head moved aside as if with impatience. My fingers stole beneath the fabric and found a moist intimation of heaven where hair fluttered from spongy flesh. Teasing apart spider webs, I found silk—had an epiphany of woman as the proper setting for man. I put it in her. I loved watching it bridge our bodies as it went in.

And she was awake and *there*, grinding up at me as I drilled into her, climaxing with a cry of *"I love you, Gary."*

With her I imagine at first it was really about Jack, about anger, revenge and validation. But that soon passed. From the start I think I understood her, how her fear I'd think her a slut would cleave her to me, transform her emotion into the banner of true love she still upholds. I think we understood each other.

And after all, the body doesn't lie. In our animal selves we show the same candor as other animals, and the animal facts never let us down. The allure of men for me had been some seeming correspondence of their characters to their genitals. I admire strength and autonomy, and falsely associated them with the penis. But now I'd matured enough not to insist on the appearance, but to rely on the *fact*. I could relish the softness of Briana's body precisely because she's stronger than any man I ever met.

Only as a mother does a man *need* a woman, but after that night, as I came forward to wrestle from the world what I wanted from it, I knew I had a partner.

I'm speaking of my wife, so shall say no more. Obviously, many years have passed, and we've gone through a great deal together—not all of it good, for how could that be? But our relationship endures because it continues to grow. It's a journey of mutual discovery.

21.

A FEW DAYS LATER, on summer's first meltingly hot day, I was pushing my Spyder, top down, across the rolling countryside south of Siena. Where the road crossed the Elsa River, I pulled off, wanting to see for myself where from time immemorial the Sienese have gone in the summertime to bathe.

Cars were parked along a dirt track, along with a half dozen mopeds. I followed a path across sloping sheep-speckled meadows to a fringe of plane trees, beneath which a sheet of silver water rippled. Twenty yards wide, it was shallow, slow-moving and had a fine grassy bank. On this weekday morning there were only a few families splashing or lying in the sun—men in the briefest of suits, meant more to project than to cover their genitals, women in thongs watching over infants who cavorted in a state of nature. It was idyllic.

Instinct drew me along a narrower path downriver, around a bend, then another. I came within sight of faster water, sheltered by taller trees and a steeper bank. The water was shaded, but the sun picked out the naked bodies of four or five teenage boys lying along its verge. Others splashed in the river, joshing one another comfortably. In town these same boys wore shapeless coats and shirts pulled down firmly over their tails. Here they lounged in the freedom and equality of nudity, casting off their shyness with their clothes. Why not, when clothes represent shame?

Sunlight mercilessly exposed their torsos and gilded their pubic regions. There, in black nests, lolled red-beaked shafts that put me in mind of birds feeding. The lean irreducibility of the male body expresses the masculine principle; its beauty is precisely that it's utilitarian, the skin barely sufficing to encase bone and muscle: Its very structure serves as sole ornament.

Well, perhaps it does have one other, like a flower on a stalk.

I sat down at a distance, drew up my knees, for some time watched unnoticed.

Inevitably the scene reminded me of Michelangelo's drawings of the *Battle of Cascina*, Florentine warriors relaxing nude and disarmed alongside the Arno an instant before the Pisan ambush.

No enemy here, except the distant cries of mothers correcting their children. Those on the bank stood up—hands on hips, bellies slung in flat outward arches, faintly pregnant with their own decline—thinking of a plunge. So frail! Their beautiful faces made me wonder how much the alluringly liquid Italian cast of feature owes to the African slaves who at the fall of Rome made up its majority. I wished I had binoculars, but the sun flashing on them would mean I'd see nothing more than blurred asses lolloping into the water with jeers of *"Finochio!"*—and possibly rocks—aimed my way. Unfair; my enjoyment was purely aesthetic.

One boy crouched to dive, then suddenly stood up tall, muscles plating his midsection. Shaking hair out of his face, he shaded his eyes and looked straight at me.

My solitary figure, moisture beginning to seep into my seat, must have looked pathetic. I was not one of them. This was their place, not mine. I got up and went back to my car. Michelangelo's drawings have a tinge of melancholy, too: Those backs flex, those genitals arch not for his pleasure. On paper they stand as distinctly apart from him as those youths on the riverbank did from me. Pornographers must be the loneliest of men (not that I'm calling Michelangelo a pornographer).

By some association of ideas I was put in mind of the Battle of Montaperti, where in 1260 the Sienese for once routed the Florentines, and I drove vaguely in the direction of that battlefield, Siena rising conical to my left as I circled northeast. In the fields were numerous little tumuli, probably unexcavated Etruscan tombs. Coming around a turn I found Jack standing across the road, nearly invisible in a cypress's dense shadow.

I stopped.

"*Smile*, stranger," I called. "Want a lift?"

"Not from you."

"Oh, come on, Jack."

He started walking. I turned around and kept pace.

"Don't be such a kid. It's miles back to town, and I don't see anyone else on this road."

"Beggars must be choosers," he shot back.

"Look, Jack, let's talk. Semester's ending, we've been through a lot. Things don't have to end this badly."

He strode ahead in grim, punishing silence.

"If you think I've done anything wrong, I apologize," I offered. "I'm *sorry*."

His steps slowed, I swung the door open, he got in, I sticked it into gear and we began to fly along.

What is it about motion? Jack unburdened himself. It all came pouring out. He told me everything that had gone on since Rome. I asked questions and got comprehensive answers. As he talked I feinted towards Siena and away again half a dozen times. Would he be spilling everything if he were not still interested? Was there not one scene left to play? I'm only human—not above taking something offered me if it does no harm to others. Understand, Briana and I as yet had made no commitment to each other.

At random I pulled off onto a dirt road and buzzed uphill—climbing, it turned out, to one of Siena's outlying medieval fortresses.

"Like driving into the *Mona Lisa*," Jack remarked.

A stone tower drew itself up with a distinct batter, battlements biting at the sky. The huge, arched door was made up of massive planks bound with iron straps.

"Let's check it out," I said. "See if we can get inside."

Lifting the knocker, I struck: *Bam! Bam! Bam!* It resounded with unexpected amplification.

High overhead a young woman threw open shutters. "*Che c'è?*" she called pleasantly.

"*Buon giorno*," I said, and with chartered American naïveté asked, "*È questo castello un museo?*"

She laughed. No, not a museum, she told us, but we were welcome to enjoy the garden terraces.

"*Grazie tante.*"

No sooner were we strolling along boxwood and ilex than Jack asked, "Just tell me why? Why drop me? Why bother Briana?"

"*Um.* If you recall, Jack, I think *you* dropped *me*."

"Well, you didn't want—"

"I never loved you, and never said I did," I reminded him. "I do love Briana, or at least I'm falling in love with her. We might get married. I've grown up at last."

"The proof being you're doing something against nature?"

"Against *nature?*"

"*Your* nature."

"I'll be the judge of that, thank you," I told him. "Nothing like a new background to see what and who you are. Isn't that the whole group's experience? Too bad you didn't take advantage of being here to open your eyes and think about things."

We sat down on a bench.

"I won't tell her, Gary, but you should."

"Tell her what?"

Disappointed, his eyes left mine and focused on Siena, four or five miles away and rising up like the illustration to a fairy tale. Midway, her wall cinched her in, squeezed her taller. It interested me to see from this new angle the three hills vying with one another. The sun, chased in slow motion by marmoreal clouds gliding westward, was beginning to descend. The town looked carved in depth from the richest materials.

Sun glanced off Jack's tender young ear so brightly that for a moment I thought he had an earring.

"I want to know that you're all right," I said.

"*I'm* all right," he said, managing marvelous disdain.

"So you're staying in Europe?"

"No, changed my mind. I'm going home."

"How come?"

"A lot of things."

He told me how, one day, he'd walked through some town, Todi or Gubbio, and seen kids his age making anti-American placards by hooking the letters *USA* into each other to make swastikas.

"Made me so angry, but Lord knows I've had enough *Mensa* arguments about American imperialism to last a lifetime. Funny, Italians seem to accept things the way they are so long as they get theirs along the edges. Our country's a lot less corrupt, I think. Anyway, implicit in the idea of America is removal from elsewhere. My ancestors made a clean break of it, and I mean to honor that. I want to go home."

"Probably the best place for you," I offered.

We contemplated the city.

"You can read it from here, Jack," I said. "It's the very

figure of the medieval mind: Nature at the bottom—woods and fields—then barns, gas stations, a factory or two, houses—secular things. At the top, churches reach for heaven, especially the highest of them all, the *Duomo*—though notice how its bell tower and the *Torre del Mangia* reach the exact same height?

"It's the medieval view, Jack, but not an inaccurate cross-section of the way things are even today. The European view may not be ours, quite, but it stands the test of time. The world was here before either of us, and it'll be here after us, too. Do like me—find your place in it. And do it soon: In ten years, you won't be so cute."

"Gary, I'm ready for whatever may come. I'm out of a made-up world and living in the real one. *You* I've survived. I only hope Briana does."

My amusement apparently annoyed him.

"You have to *care*, Gary," he informed me. "Caring about *people* and what happens to them is the only theory by which life can mean anything."

Oh, youth's capacity for drama! For self-importance! For believing its own publicity!

"Well, Jack, just as when the Romans copied a Greek original—"

He *exploded*. "Gary, all your comebacks, your fucking *art, art, art* is shit you throw at life—armor to keep it from *touching* you. Art's more real to you than life could ever be!"

"You don't care for my stylish carapace?"

Searching my face, Jack sighed one unhappy sigh and turned away.

"Sometimes the best you can hope for," I murmured, placing my hand on his knee, "is to get away from things for an afternoon."

So far, so good. My hand traveled the soft denim of his

inner thigh. His legs spread. He turned his face and opened his lips with a sad little setting aside of his head. Nostalgically I kissed him.

Why does having sex outdoors make you think you're getting to the root of the matter? We moved to a hidden spot in a line of olive trees and Jack gave me suckle of that fine Greek-Gothic appendage of his. I kneeled in a rite I'd renounced but remembered, and gave him his effusive, delicious seizure.

"I like you so much," he said as he zipped up, "except you're such a *stronzo*."

"Bit harsh?" I said, unzipping. "My turn."

And he swaggered away! Tossed his shaggy head and walked off!

I almost laughed. He *had* changed. I sat in the shade watching him move down the hillside while clouds smudged thumbprints across the sky and tessellated the view of Siena. I rubbed myself, feeling something I didn't know how to name, something that for once reminded me of nothing else. I saw Jack reach the road and a car stop a minute later, saw him stoop into it and be carried away.

Then my seed pumped in arcs beneath the trees.

22.

THE GROUP OFFICIALLY disbanded the next evening with the *festa* the Donatos tossed at their villa in the Chianti Hills. Jack gave it a miss, nor did I see him again (nor do I know his fate: I fear even to Google him, for I don't see how, given his practices, he could have survived the Age of AIDS). There was no single charter flight home. Most of the girls traveled around some before returning to the U.S., though others stayed over to see the first *Palio* on July 2.

The *Palio* is Siena's famous spectacle, a centuries-old horse race run twice each summer around the circumference of the *Campo*.

Briana and I missed July's, for we were exploring the Veneto and Alto Adige. Returning to Siena at the start of August, we took a villa for the month a mile out, the Via Roma apartment having been let, as always, to musicians in the Accademia Chigiana's summer program. On August 9, as our afternoon sky was arming itself for the long bloody battle that would churn the glare of day to the black of night, we watched a snowy live image of Nixon walking to his helicopter, turning around to mimic its rotor like a spastic child, and vanish into history. A strange mood washed over the Tuscan countryside. It disconcerted Italians to see Nixon booted for reasons that couldn't scratch out a foothold in their minds: Abuse power? How do you *do* that?

Although it punctured our bubble, the lovely no-news quality of being abroad, Watergate's climax opened the sluices of health; aptly named, that cleansing cycle. It washed away crimes, evil motives, cynicism, rottenness, hypocrisy. Nixon gone, we walked away from Viet Nam and no more was heard about love and peace. People got down to real things. If foremost among them was making money, what's more human or of more benefit to the race?

It was time to go home, but first we wanted to witness the summer's second *Palio*, on August 16.

23.

SIENA IS DIVIDED INTO 13 *contrade*. My old flat being in the *contrada del Leocorno* ("Unicorn"), Briana and I were welcomed to the first part of *Leocorno*'s feast on the eve of the *Palio*: pasta, wine, banter and a core quality of something sacred. Then we were affectionately escorted out and the real party began. That polite removal prepared us for the passions manifest in the running of the race. We were, in the end, only American tourists.

To watch it we splurged on places at a trefoil window high over Bar Costa. It cost us a cool hundred bucks apiece, despite the meals we'd eaten there, the big tips we'd left. Regardless. We got there early and hung over the sill, watching 100,000 people pack themselves into the middle of the *Campo*, separated from the periphery's track of new-laid clay by temporary wooden barriers.

The first event of the pre-race *Corte Storico* was the flag-throwing competition each *contrada*'s prettiest boys perform in

Renaissance tights and doublets. Some of the tights resembled droopy long johns; undarned holes showed what color underwear the kids were wearing (or not). To brisk drum tattoos, they whipped their flags high into the air, catching them and tossing them again in synchronized patterns, before rotating onwards and doing it again.

Then bands blaring marches paraded, stopping to play haunting bits from opera. Men bearing the winning *contrade*'s prize—the *palio*, a newly painted silk banner depicting Mary of the Assumption—followed the bands, making a circuit of the *Campo* before the gaze of the townspeople.

Officials cleared a path and after a stage wait a troop of mounted *carabinieri* filed into the *Campo* in a line that filled the track's width. They walked once around it in stately fashion as the crowd began a rumble that built steadily. At their second lap the *carabinieri* began to trot smartly, standing in their stirrups with sabers raised straight up over their heads. Very picturesque. For the third lap, they crouched low, sabers thrust forward, and charged in an unholy lethal mass that unlocked everybody's throat. Never had I heard such a roar! Any who leaned out to see what thunder was coming risked getting his head sliced off.

The time had come for the dirtiest horse race in the world, and the noise did not diminish. Each *contrada*'s entry came in to partisan cheers. They were a motley lot, ranging from wide-hipped draft animals to beautiful Arab stallions, most in various stages of dopedness and mounted by an assortment of street thugs. Even during their ceremonial entrance riders were flailing at one another and one another's mounts with switches and fists. (Jockeys can make a fortune on that race, especially the ones bribed to throw it.)

Eventually they bundled behind the starting line, while the crowd kept up the rawest exhalation imaginable and wave after wave of emotion swept the *Piazza del Campo*.

Boom! The *mortaretto* fired and the race began.

A roiling mass, not rapid but punching, kicking, backing and turning, moved around the *Campo*. It's three times around, first horse over the line wins, even if he's left his rider behind. "YAAAAAH!" everyone yelled. "YAAAAAAAAAAH!" The horses got around the first time almost accidentally, riders stopping to slug it out, banging at the barriers.

But they got down to business in the second go-round, plunging ahead, going *fast*.

And in the last lap they accelerated, dashing as a mass hell-for-leather into the final curve, where seven or eight collided, flinging red paint over the clay and exposing gleaming white bone. Riders flew and horses went down. Moments later the *smack!* of meat into meat arrived at our window, along with the screaming.

It was horrible. Leaning out, I saw two riders lying unnaturally still. It happened to be the worst accident in years; two horses were destroyed, a jockey died, another was paralyzed. Still the crowd kept up its "YAAAAAAAH!" of blood lust; prolonged its mass orgasm until the *mortaretto* burst again to declare the race won (by *Selva*—"woods," like the "*selva oscura*" where Dante has his mid-life crisis at the start of *The Divine Comedy*).

Fascinating, this stylized slaughter. Unbelievable that mortal suffering was taking place in the midst of pageantry not a hundred yards away. Briana just kind of refused to take it in. She backed away from the window and clasped her arms around herself, until she had to stop her ears against the horses' agony. I've never been able to drag her to another *Palio*. But it was exhilarating to witness a tradition kept up not as a tourist exhibition but the real thing, authentic emotion still attached.

A few days later we returned to Washington, where I wrote my letter of resignation from Adams U. and set out in the middle of a recession to find a museum job. But I was resolved to tear myself away from that academic life of least resistance. After nerve-wracking months, during which Briana's shifts at the student cafeteria were of material help, an offer came through as junior-under-assistant-curator at the National Gallery.

I rolled up my sleeves and got to work.

So did all of us, and the rest is history; history, and quite a ride. Of course, self-interest loosed the true voice of my generation, and a lot of repellent characters crawled out of the woodwork. To this day Baby Boomers have never left infancy behind—our sense of entitlement, our appetites, our fierce possessiveness and judgmental mutual jealousy still fly high. Self-regard drowns out everything; if it hasn't happened to a Boomer, it's never happened in history.

That first job was the making of me. Through an unlikely series of events it placed me on the road that brought me to where I sit today, gazing into a Pacific sunset as Founding Director of The Constance Collection, the famous museum complex above Santa Barbara built by microchip megabucks, where I recycle stupendous money-making for the benefit of art, transubstantiate cash into masterpieces.

It took a lot for me to leave the academy, but I wanted to risk myself in a larger field, compete for richer rewards. And it's worked out better than I dreamed. Mr. Constance long ago made me a multi-millionaire. He said (and he's a man of insight) that I had to be someone he could respect if I were to build his collection. But the satisfaction's been so great I would willingly have paid *him*. The Constance Collection, so largely my creation, permits two million visitors a year to experience the beauty and passion of the greatest art. And I sense that I may be at the threshold of a larger future still.

Behind a man of accomplishment there usually stands the woman who prevented him from doing more. Not so Briana; I could not have had my career without her.

Every year we get back to where it began for us for a few restorative weeks. More and more Siena resembles those women who have work done and go about with auras strained and unnatural. The cats and pigeons are long gone, along with the peasants and poverty. But though the town may be less artlessly old than she used to be, her essence endures. She remains our relationship's matrix and spiritual home, our time there part of the quiet life Briana cherishes.

Only last month, after a week of auctions in London, we alighted for replenishment at the pied-à-terre we bought before prices rose, happily chancing upon a concert — Arnaldo Cohen playing Rachmaninoff — at the Accademia Chigiana.

The Chigiana's concert chamber is a grandly decorated but intimate room framed by pilasters of Siena marble, that yellow stone instinct with red forms struggling to emerge. Venetian mirrors hang between them, enormous productions 300 years old whose gilt frames writhe around blistered surfaces. Some quality in them hallows the light and mutes the colors. Their reflectivity could be called imperfect, save that by virtually a Jamesian dispensation they possess a penetrating psychology that varnishes their scenes in a lapidary reality. As we listened I chanced to look aside and, through tears wrung by Rachmaninoff, saw two crackled images floating in contentment, a man and woman united by time's arrow-shot of inevitability.

But then my eyes met those of a youth sitting behind us with the confident, self-conscious presence of a Bronzino — virtually the double of myself at his age. His face, held at a rigid angle, raw with hunger, contrasted with mine, burnished by time and satiated with wisdom. Once I might have projected back a silent complicity. No longer, of course. Instead I pushed out my lips as though I had a bad taste in my mouth, as though to say, "You're mistaken about *me*." Resuming the snug, tough mask that his boldness perhaps for an instant dislodged, I studied my wife's countenance in the mirror's dusky depths. It must have been the music, but she looked entangled in the nets of time, wreathed in grief like Mary in Michelangelo's *Pietà*.

I patted her hand and, a cough threatening, reached into my pocket for a mint, glancing again at the youth. His eyes burned unblinking. I gave the slightest of nods—let him parse its meaning as he would!—unwrapped the mint and lightly, proudly touched Briana's knee. She turned for a moment, brows knit in reproof of the wrapper's noise. I placed the mint in my mouth—and choked.

Standing up quietly, hand to my throat, I made my way to the men's room, careful not to disturb her further.

The Man Who Owned New York

*For Nathan Micajah Key (1850-1890),
my great-grandfather,
whose bones were raised from his grave
on the high Texas plains in 1922
and sacrificed to his descendants' vain efforts
to prove themselves heirs
to Manhattan's fabulous "Edwards Estate"*

Money will arrange matters in New York, *that* I know.

                                        Theodore Dreiser, *The Titan*

1.

EDITH WHARTON DIED the other day.

I always wondered what she made of him the Press 30 years ago dubbed *The Man Who Owned New York,* and regretted that she never treated of his sensational story in her nuanced fiction. Now she never will. But an outlander (and one with a beautiful daughter) fighting for the colossal Manhattan real-estate fortune stolen from his forebears, the sanctimonious squatters wheeling up their legal artillery, while the city's social bastions rock in resistance and capitulation — Wharton would have made a great thing of it. Even Henry James might have found sufficiently evocative the return to New York of a Tory family exiled since the Revolutionary War in the person of a rangy Kansas farmer.

Now James and Wharton both have gone without making use of him or his story. If it's not to be forgotten, it seems left to me. I was there, a figure on the periphery but placed so as to see the whole, and it happened that I — or rather, my crime *(oh, my gaudy crime!)* — resolved the episode. An account will also serve as my spiritual autobiography, for without *The Man Who Owned New York* I might never have found my own true path.

IT WAS A PULL at the doorbell that precipitated me into the affair.

The doorbell in question belonged to the rectory of All Angels, the old church that stoppers the maw of Wall Street at Broadway. At 11:00 o'clock of the forenoon, on Wednesday, November 6, 1907, in only the second month of my first (and decidedly plum) parish assignment, I was at my desk outside Father Day's office. Supposedly I was double-checking his calculations for a Greenwich Street store lease, but in truth I was admiring how fallen leaves complement crumbling grave markers, their soft, sodden colors melting into the half-dissolved stone. Perhaps I was also daydreaming about my future; five weeks in it proved New York the loneliest place I'd ever known.

Then the doorbell rang.

Usually Mrs. Brown or one of her maids answered it, but for some reason *I* bounded downstairs. Through the etched glass I saw the silhouette of a man wearing a homburg hat. Intending to send him round to the tradesmen's entrance in back, I opened the door and from the side came a frightening white flash: *Floomp!* The photographer retreated down the steps with his contraption, while the man in the homburg said, "Father Day?"

"What is this? Who are you? Did that man take my *photograph?*"

"Hopkins of *The World*," he replied, naming the city's most scurrilous newspaper. "May I come in, Father Day?"

"The rector is busy," I said. "I'm Father Stackpole, his secretary, and *no*, you may *not* come in."

"All right, Rover Boy, all right," said Hopkins. "Keep your shirt on."

My voice shook as I repeated my name, for his spontaneous appellation infuriated me. Heroes of juvenile fiction, the Rover Boys were the epitome of clean-cut, blue-eyed, manly all-American youth, resourceful foes of wrongdoers and miscreants. And *Dick Rover* happened to have been my nickname at Groton, Yale, even Divinity. In my schooldays I took it in good part—behind the mockery lay envy, especially of my playing-field prowess—but as an ordained minister of the cloth I thought it impertinence coming from a stranger.

"Well, Reverend, Mr. Denton Slaughter of Ellinwood, Kansas came by *The World* this morning to tell us how All Angels Church stole his family's farm in Manhattan more than a century ago. According to him, everything your church *says* it owns really belongs to *him*, and he's here to collect."

"Stuff and nonsense!" I snapped with disdain. *Floomp!* "Good *day*, gentlemen."

"Thanks, Dick," said Hopkins as I slammed the door shut.

I returned upstairs and reported the incident to Father Day, ending by asking, "Could there be any truth to such a claim?"

Rocking his chair back, Father Day removed the green eyeshade he customarily wore at his desk. Stroking the black eye thus revealed (suffered, he told me, kneeling in private devotions), he sought the answer in the opulence of his office, which like the rest of the rectory resembled an exclusive men's club. Its walls were paneled in walnut, Tiffany windows muffled Broadway's noise, there was a bronze Saint-Gaudens overmantel, a choice Burne-Jones *Holy Family* and gleaming mahogany furniture made by the Herter Brothers.

Sighing, he joined his palms in a steeple atop the dome of his stomach.

"Exactly *how* All Angels comes to be so richly endowed, we cannot know with certainty, Albert," he pronounced.

"Tradition tells us it's to Queen Anne's munificence we're beholden, but the exact truth seems lost to the mists of time."

"Yes, Father, but—"

"Never mind that we work like slaves to make proper eleemosynary use of it, naturally our property makes us a target for every kind of sharper. The person you speak of is evidently one of them, unless, indeed, he's but the dupe of a larger conspiracy."

"Yes, but if—"

"Money and property go, in the end, to the virtuous. That is the happy truth on which our country is founded, Albert—why America comes every day closer to being the earthly paradise."

"But—"

The steeple collapsed and Father Day's manner took on the austerity that reminded me he would one day be a bishop. Rocking his stocky body forward, he clapped the eyeshade to his brow and reached for the ground lease he'd been marking up when I interrupted.

"Father Stackpole, we have work to do!"

2.

OVER THE SOUP at lunch, I braved Father Day's frown to relate my Press encounter to our colleagues, Fathers Andrews and Morris.

"'Stuff and nonsense,' I told them, and they left."

"How on earth could such a notion arise?" asked Father Morris with a sniff.

"Isn't this a claim that recurs?" suggested corpulent Father Andrews, who had been at All Angels since before I was born.

"There are indeed occasional letters," Father Day confirmed. "Missives scrawled from such places as *Iowa* or *Ohio*—however you pronounce it—claiming ownership of our demesne on the basis of obscure family legends."

"How do we respond to them?" I asked.

"Why, they go to Sullivan & Cromwell, of course," he answered, naming our attorneys. "How *they* shut them up, I have no idea. But they do it. Rest assured, what All Angels possesses no pretended claimant will tear away from it."

"*Laches*," murmured Father Andrews.

"*Laches?*" I repeated. "What an odd word. What does it mean?"

In silence a maid removed the soup bowls, and Mrs. Brown herself placed the roast before Father Day. Lunch was our most substantial meal. The rector complimented Mrs. Brown, then answered my question before taking up the more congenial task of carving.

"*Laches* means the right to dispute someone's possession of property lapses with time. In New York State, I believe after 15 years."

"Unless possession is due to fraud," noted Father Andrews, "in which case there is no—*um*—statute of limitations."

Father Day's knife and fork clattered to the tabletop, and he stared balefully.

"The matter is *moot*," he said, uttering the *t* in so final a manner as to spray the roast. "It's true there's an unfortunate murkiness to the record. During the Revolutionary War, confusion reigned, for even as George Washington was expelling the British from the city, our Episcopalian predecessors were giving the boot to the Church of England. And the fire of 1793 destroyed not only the church but its archives. But though we cannot document exactly *how* All Angels comes to own 200 acres of lower Manhattan, after 125 years' uninterrupted possession, and in the absence of any evidence of wrongdoing, we are *quite* safe."

Father Day resumed carving and we passed the plates. As we ate, he reverted more cheerfully to his favorite topic.

"As I was telling Albert this morning, money—land—*property* have a natural affinity for the good. They come to us as though they know the way by heart. And thank goodness for it! Only last week, Morgan was able to stop the Panic—save the *country*—by advancing the Treasury 50 million from his own pocket! The affinity of money to virtue, to *power*, is *most* beneficial to society."

He shook his head in admiration. How he would have loved to have J.P. Morgan as a parishioner! But Morgan, alas, was faithful to the Stuyvesant Square congregation of St. George's.

"There are seeming exceptions," he continued, "rich men who appear villainous. But as if by magic—though really by the iron laws of economics—money works its transformative powers. For example, rough tales are told of Mr. Rockefeller in the Pennsylvania oil fields years ago—but see him today! The sweetest, most philanthropic gentleman! I regret that he worships with the Baptists, but that is his affair. And Mr. Carnegie! Quite the rapscallion in his time, they say, but today so rich and generous!

"This affinity brings us heavy duties, to be sure. As the good amass ever more wealth, so increases the irksomeness of finding ways of using it for the benefit of those we have always with us—to wit, the poor. It's our duty to do so, however—to a due degree: Not so much as to impede wealth's multiplication, which its concentration so materially assists."

He paused to chew and swallow.

"We need merely look about us to see this concentration of wealth expressed in the skyscrapers lifting our neighborhood higher year by year (closer to heaven, as I like to think), until—how tall is the Singer Building to be?"

The skeleton of the Singer Building's new tower clawed at the sky a few blocks to the north. Widening on high like a torchiere, it already rose higher than the Flatiron Building, previously tallest in the world.

"Forty-seven stories," I offered.

"*For*-ty *sev*-en *sto*-ries!" sang Father Day. "On land leased from All Angels for 99 years. I negotiated the deal myself, though of course the Vestry reviewed it. Over the next century the Singer Building will produce *millions* with which to carry on our good works."

"More churches?" I asked. "More chapels?"

"Above all, the new Cathedral of St. John the Divine, the largest gothic church in the world!"

There was a pause before Father Morris inquired, "But, Father Day, are the poor to blame for their poverty? Surely it takes money to make money?"

"More proof of its love for the good!" retorted the rector. "Its growth amplifies the original, hard-won results of enterprise.

"Only the other day our Warden, Mr. Shoatsbury, was telling me about *his* start in business. Seems he was a Western Union boy in the day before stock tickers—the fastest lad in New York—and whenever news came in, he ran it like the wind to its destination, no matter the weather, and eventually his effort caught someone's eye, and so on and so forth. He happened to mention that his net worth today exceeds *one hundred million dollars.* A better man I never met."

That afternoon I was drafting routine letters raising office rents on Fulton Street when I heard Father Day's private telephone ring repeatedly, I guessed with calls from our Vestrymen. His voice took on an edge of frustration.

He called me in.

"Albert, would you please go out and find a copy of *The World?* The extra edition."

"Certainly, Father Day."

This novel assignment *(The Herald-Tribune* and *Wall Street Journal* made up our usual budget of news) was easy to accomplish, for a newsy was bawling *"Extra! Extra!"* at the bottom of our very steps.

I handed over two cents—and goggled:

ALL ANGELS ESTATE QUESTIONED
"AM RIGHTFUL HEIR TO HEART OF CITY,"
DECLARES D. SLAUGHTER OF KANSAS
Church Theft Detailed—Enormous Wealth At Stake
Farmer Claims 200 Acres Valued At
$1,000,000,000
Billion-Dollar Inheritance Makes Man
Richest In World!

Beneath, printed in thick black strokes by the crude photographic reproduction of the day, was the picture of an enraged prig in a clerical collar. That was myself. The caption read *'Rover Boy' Throws Out Our Reporter.*

These headlines, screaming with the conviction of print, I

placed in front of Father Day.

"*Dammit,*" he ejaculated. He skimmed the articles, then quoted, with his customary hint of mockery, "'close resemblance to Dick Rover.' Indeed, Dick's the fair-haired one? All right, Albert, I'm handing this matter over to you."

"Father?"

With distaste he folded the newspaper and held it across his leather-topped desk.

"I have neither the time nor the temper, whereas this fairy tale appears to pique your curiosity, and clearly you've a rapport with the Press. Take care of it—forthwith. Father Morris can take your desk in the meantime. Nip it in the bud, is my advice."

"Father?"

In exasperation he threw the newspaper at me.

"It's all yours, Rover Boy."

3.

FINDING FATHER MORRIS in the parish house giving an English lesson, I transmitted Father Day's order.

Whereas the rectory was hushed all day but for the clean sound of typewriters worked by the dozen clerks I helped supervise, the parish house was Bedlam. There our practice of muscular Christianity came to life. Not only did it house such staff members as Mrs. Brown, her maids and housemen, the porters, our choirmaster, organist, bell-ringers and archivist, but immigrant masses from the East Side thronged it for lessons in English, housekeeping, childcare, citizenship—everything they needed in order to become decent Americans. We had a staff of social workers, but the rest of us helped out; it was parish tradition. Even Father Day took a personal interest in what he saw as the most promising young men, however threatening they might appear to the rest of us.

While Father Morris installed himself at my desk, I took *The World* up to the library and read it through. Four pages told *The Rightful Heir*'s story in dangerously plausible terms.

Denton Slaughter claimed that William and Mary had granted one Captain Micajah Slaughter—a *pirate*, forsooth!—200 acres in the lower part of the Crown's new possession of Manhattan Island in gratitude for funneling gold to the royal coffers from ships of the Spanish treasure fleet he captured. Settling on his new estate, the pirate turned farmer and raised a family. Successive generations continued to work the farm, though also developing lots along Broadway (always by leasehold, never by sale), until 1783, when, as the British occupiers of New York were forced to flee, Capt. Slaughter's Loyalist descendant—one Daniel Slaughter—removed to Canada with his family. But in order to safeguard his property in his absence, before leaving town he leased his acreage for a term of ten years to his parish, All Angels.

Daniel Slaughter died in Ontario, but when his heirs returned to New York after the lapse of the lease, they found All Angels not only in firm possession of their land but refusing to relinquish it. Their manor house, moreover, was gone and their fields torn up and rapidly being covered with streets, houses, offices, stores and workshops. *The World*, citing a contemporary account in the New York *Gazette*, said the family went to law but, in retaliation for having taken the war's losing side, got no satisfaction. It was just then, in 1793, that fire destroyed the old colonial church of All Angels and its archives. No more was heard of Slaughters in New York; they were thought to have migrated west.

The World superimposed a diagram of what Denton Slaughter claimed to own over a map of the parish's holdings. They made a neat match, comprising what lies between Wall Street and Canal Street, from Broadway to the North River. Its capsule history of the parish followed that adumbrated in Father Day's pamphlet, *A Short History of All Angels Church,* which tells how English colonists founded the parish in 1699 and, after enough Indians had been killed to make it safe to tear down Wall Street's namesake barrier, raised a church "to mediate symbolically between colonists and Indians, as now it mediates between God and, as represented by the financial district, Mammon." Queen Anne, declares this account, granted the young parish 200 acres and, although the parchment recording her largesse was lost in the fire, the land had been held from that time forward and developed by a succession of shrewd rectors so that All Angels became — as it remained — New York's richest landowner.

The World even diagrammed our complex. The churchyard abutting the ample rectory boasted the tombs of Founders and Signers, while to the church's other side stood the six-story parish house. After the first church burned, no one knows how, it was rebuilt as the brownstone structure that survives today.

And above the caption *The Man Who Owns New York* appeared Denton Slaughter's photograph. It showed a raw-boned man of 50 or 55, his face distinguished by a flourishing white mustache and the jutting cheekbones usual to Midwestern farmers, as if stolen from the Indians they displaced. His expression radiated dignity.

When finally I laid the newspaper down, I was startled to find it getting dark outside. For some time past I'd been unconsciously aware of footfalls below, of low exchanges in the kinds of voices reserved for serious occasions. Suddenly Father Day banged open the oaken door and said, "Albert! Where have you been? I've been looking everywhere. The Vestry's here!"

"Father?"

"A special meeting! You are wanted!"

4.

TAKING THE STEPS two at a time, I ran down to the Vestry Room. In cold blood the prospect of appearing before the city's most rapacious businessmen, especially a tad out of breath, would have terrified me, but there was no time now to be scared, though I confess to hesitating at the door when I saw the fierce old heads that lined the table. "Not the first man to think he owns New York," grumbled one. Growled his neighbor, "That damn Morgan."

Catching up to me, Father Day pushed me inside the room.

"Gentlemen, this is my new secretary, Albert Stackpole, who is to be the face of All Angels in this matter," he announced. "I'm sure you'll agree it's a sincere and guileless face, apt to make a good appearance for us."

"Hear, hear," several grunted.

Father Day receded to the side of the room, leaving me standing at the table's end. Presiding opposite, from the chair specially built to withstand his bulk, wheezed the very image of immobility. Mustaches, eyebrows and sideburns dyed auburn licked like flames around the gleaming gimlet eyes of Cornelius Shoatsbury, Warden of All Angels and Wall Street magnate of the first rank. This head, otherwise bald, was the cherry atop the sundae of flesh lapping over his chair; the boy runner had vanished.

"Sit down, Father Stackpole, *if* you please!" he boomed. He sounded annoyed I hadn't thought of doing it myself.

I took my seat facing him, and he formally started the meeting. It was novel to see Mr. Archer, who fought his way to control of three railroads one step ahead of two grand juries, mildly reading minutes of the last meeting. As he droned on I looked around the table, but even my mildest glance happening to alight upon a Vestryman roused alert nods or twirls of the mustache or animal flashes of the eye. Behind Shoatsbury blazed John LaFarge's great window, a radiant *Parable of the Talents* depicting a city of towers flourishing above a flaming gold piece, which coin served—or so it looked from my end of the table—as Shoatsbury's halo.

"Thanks, Archer," he said. "Gentlemen, I called this special meeting in response to the *fantastical* story splashed across *The World* this afternoon. A *farmer* from *Kansas* has the *effrontery* to claim we stole his family's land, *lo*, these many years ago?" He snorted. "Stand up, Father Stackpole, and tell us your plan of action!"

"Well, I haven't formed a plan—" I began, working to my feet.

"First thing you should have done," snapped Shoatsbury, to a murmur of agreement. "Can't proceed without a plan!"

"I've read what *The World* says—"

"Yes, yes, we've all seen it," Shoatsbury growled.

"Let him go on," suggested Father Day.

"First, I suggest we look into Slaughter's account—search the archives for Queen Anne's grant."

"Nonsense! Archives were picked clean years ago," barked Shoatsbury. "So you assured *me*, Father Day."

"No, no, there's nothing dangerous to us there," murmured the rector. "The fire of 1793 took care of that. By the same token, of course, we're deprived of evidence to rebut this would-be usurper. By all means glance through the archives, Albert, but a thorough search is *quite* unnecessary."

"My dear Father Stackpole, I think I see your point," broke in Mr. Archer, "and I'm ashamed to tear an energetic young priest like yourself away from parish duties to deal with this absurd threat. You must think it a waste of time."

"Not at all, Mr. Archer," I replied staunchly. "I'm here to do my best for the parish—whatever its Vestry and Father Day ask of me."

Dark and meager Mr. Seyforth, partner in Sullivan & Cromwell, spoke up in his emollient manner.

"I suggest you visit this farmer, Father Stackpole," he said. "Tell him we will fight tooth-and-nail to keep what belongs to us, that we have the means to do it, and make him know, also, that we love to fight. Hint that the law punishes those who make false claims on other people's property.

"Whatever the historical merits of Slaughter's claim," Seyforth continued, addressing the table at large, "equity aids the vigilant—*not* men like this farmer, who by the best construction is a procrastinator beyond compare: There applies the legal doctrine of *laches*."

"Unless—" I suggested. "Unless our possession is due to fraud?"

The resulting silence embarrassed me. It was as though I'd

introduced a rude smell.

"No fraud can be proved in this case," said Seyforth at last. "Slaughter family tradition unaccompanied by legal proofs will not prevail in court. I don't necessarily dispute the farmer's good faith, but what may be *probable* is not, in my judgment, *provable*."

"I think, Mr. Seyforth, we need not concede even your *'probable,'* for fear of confusing Father Stackpole," interposed Father Day, his eyes on me. "Albert, the case is open and shut: This man wants what's ours and must therefore be *squelched*."

"I'm sure there's no need to worry," said Seyforth, removing his pince-nez and sending his cold eyes around the table, "possession being, as is said, nine-tenths of the law. But we must mount a forceful defense, lest the Press whip up public opinion to our discomfiture."

Shoatsbury said darkly, "What I want to know is, who is *behind* this?"

"Our supposition has long been that there exists a ring of sharpers," said Seyforth, "possibly in this very city, that recruits supposed 'heirs' so as to mulct them for 'fees' and 'expenses' in regard to some fictitious lawsuit for some factitious recovery. I confess that having one come to town is new. Perhaps this man Slaughter grew impatient with the stately pace of the ring's efforts."

"Outrageous!" said the Warden. "A man works his fingers to the bone his whole life, trying to put by a few pennies for his old age, and a *farmer* from *Kansas* thinks he'll get *rich* merely by showing up? A promotion swindle of the rankest kind!"

"Gentlemen, we must uphold the rights of property!" proclaimed one Vestryman.

Another: "Who is safe, should this claim succeed?"

"Next the Indians will claim Manhattan Island!"

"The whole country!"

"It won't do, won't do at *all*," said Mr. Archer, launching a pious litany. "All Angels does *much* good."

"The Cathedral rises with funds we contribute!"

"Morningside University stands a monument to our gifts!"

"The Home for Incorrigibles is *ours!*"

"The Home for Unwed Mothers: *Ours!*"

"The Unfortunates of the Streets: Our very *own!*"

"Yes, yes, gentlemen, this is all very well," interrupted Shoatsbury, "but one cannot deny there's something to the sound of *one billion dollars* that might inflame public passions."

He aimed his porcine snout at me. It was second in size, inflammation and fame only to Morgan's own proboscis.

"It's up to you, Father Stackpole," he declared, the fierce pig eyes boring in on me. "Show some moxie: Go see this farmer and *scare* him."

"Yes, Mr. Shoatsbury, I will!"

"Don't let us down."

"No, sir."

Dismissed, I stood up and left the room. Behind me I heard the parliamentary niceties of ending the meeting.

5.

THE VESTRY'S EXHORTATIONS working on me like a locker-room pep talk, I ran out of that room boiling for a fight! My indignation surged — to think of anyone trying to gull All

Angels!—as I donned my overcoat and looked for my muffler.

Father Day, however, bidding Vestrymen goodbye, broke into laughter as I rushed for the door. He insisted I eat dinner before leaving to bell the lion in his den.

Accordingly, I wolfed my food in front of my scandalized colleagues, and ignored their conversation about the expediency of pulling down Federal mansions on Vesey Street for a new office building; my mission was vastly more important. I shocked Mrs. Brown by refusing her bread pudding and, Father Day's nod giving me permission, bolted.

Even at that hour, I had to brush past clamoring reporters on the rectory's stoop before ducking beneath the iron clamshell that gave entry to the Inter-Borough Railway. The subway train rattled me up the rails with flashes of lightning and a roar that promised delivery to hell.

At Seventh Avenue and 23rd Street I got off and walked east, to where Broadway slices the corner off Madison Square at Fifth Avenue. There loomed the distinguished seven stories which, according to *The World,* sheltered our nemesis: The Fifth Avenue Hotel. Host to Wilde and Twain and the Prince of Wales, it had been New York's leading hostelry for half a century; its luster was recently dimmed by the new Waldorf ten blocks farther uptown, but apparently Slaughter preferred to stay nearer his "farm."

To my eye its marble exterior resembled a London hotel's, but the double-storied lobby could belong nowhere but New York. It buzzed with activity. Powerful men, smoking and spitting and talking about their money, occupied chairs and couches; great ladies perched on ottomans and settees, pretending to be oblivious to the talk. Uniformed servitors flitted through to a never-ending chiming of bells and ringing of telephones and slamming of cash-register drawers.

At the front desk I asked Slaughter's room number.

"Prince of Wales suite, top floor," said the exquisitely bored clerk, snapping bright-nailed fingers for a bellboy to show me to the elevator.

Upstairs I traversed a silk-walled corridor and knocked at double doors.

"Coming!" called a big cheerful voice.

The door opening, I advanced into the foyer of a capacious reception room. A dozen men—reporters, among them Hopkins of *The World*—regarded me. The pinch of hands at my shoulders taking my coat unmasked me as a cleric, and I glowered, inviting all and sundry to take my measure and tremble.

And they laughed!

I preserved my countenance, however, until the attendant who opened the door and took my coat pawed at my field of vision with the largest, roughest hand I ever saw. I turned to find a tall, broad, faultlessly attired figure, extravagant white mustachios giving flight to sunburned cheekbones.

"Good evening, Reverend," said Slaughter. It was unmistakably he. "Are you from All Angels?"

"Yes, sir. My name is Albert Stackpole."

"I am Denton Slaughter."

Floomp! from the ever-ready photographers, and the morning papers had the picture they captioned *The Unanswered Handshake,* for, as our august Vestry's emissary, I didn't design to touch the farmer's fingers.

"I take it kindly of you to call, Father Stackpole," he said cordially, seemingly accepting my rudeness as a New York custom. He waved away the smoke of magnesium flash powder.

Coldly I asked, "Is there some place we can talk?"

"In here," he said. He ushered me into a sitting room that overlooked Madison Square. Across it shone the Garden;

lights picked out nude *Diana* atop it. There was mocking heathenism to the lift of her golden breasts as, like a lofty Cupid, she pointed her arrow at me. Below, men strode beneath globes of electric light along chain-bordered walks.

Closing the door, Slaughter gave *Diana* an avid glance and indicated chairs beside the windows. He sat down with a pluck at the knees of his dove-gray trousers and studied my face and hands. Mine were not the usual hands of a priest; mine had calluses enough from my years rowing crew to enable me to look any farmer in the eye.

"Mr. Slaughter, my rector Father Day and our Vestry have sent me to settle your outrageous claim."

"I was thinking myself that a settlement could save much grief at law," Slaughter sighed, stretching his legs out straight. "If we can cut across, I'm prepared to listen to a figure of—"

"I don't mean that sort of settlement, sir," I said hastily. "I simply wish to warn you that persisting with your claim will open you to a world of trouble. Do I make myself clear, sir? A *world* of trouble."

His brow tightened. "I hoped you came here to discuss the matter, Reverend, not to make threats."

"By all means, let's discuss it. You claim—"

"Here, Mr. Richard Weis of your city wrote me a letter." He handed me an envelope. "This arrived Monday, Reverend. That evening my daughter and I were on the train for New York."

I unfolded the page within. Beneath an engraved heading was typing in violet ink:

SLAUGHTER HEIRS ASSOCIATION

900 GRAND STREET
NEW YORK CITY

October 29, 1907

Mr. Denton Slaughter
Ellinwood, Kansas

Dear Mr. Slaughter,

    This is to invite you to join the Slaughter Heirs Association and help press its claim to the 200 acres of lower Manhattan, New York City, that comprise the Slaughter family farm. All Angels Church unlawfully seized the farm after the Revolutionary War and occupies it to this day. Owing to the concentration of Financial District and other buildings on it, we estimate its present value to be One Billion Dollars ($1,000,000,000).

    The purposes of the Association are to amalgamate its evidence to proofs held by family members, and to file a legal challenge to All Angels' possession, which the Association is prepared to help pursue in consideration of a small percentage of any ultimate recovery. Because large expenses are to be anticipated in unseating the church, you are urged to remit your membership fee of $50 promptly. Failure to do so will forfeit your share of the recovery.

> In addition, the Association meets next spring at the Windsor Hotel, Garden City, Kansas. Hoping you will there inscribe your name on the Roll of Heirs,
>
> I remain,

It was signed *Richard Weis*.

Contemptuously I handed it back.

"*Piffle,* Mr. Slaughter," I said. "A letter asking for money? Filled with vague claims, unspecified proofs? And you merely one of an unknown number of 'heirs'? Ludicrous!"

Eyes flashing, he declared, "I am *sole* heir, Father Stackpole: The only son of an only child, and my grandfather was the eldest of Daniel Slaughter's children."

"I didn't know primogeniture obtained in this country," I said, sneering.

"A man can leave his property where he chooses, and in my family the land descended *in toto* to the eldest son. It was kept whole and its income devoted to educating for the trades and professions those who would not inherit."

"How is it, then, that it passed out of your family's control, Mr. Slaughter?"

"Because we leased it to *your* church, Father, and when the lease expired you refused to surrender it! Just kept it! *Robbed* us, sir, at a time when we were in bad odor with the public and had no recourse except to courts that were in cahoots with you!"

"*Hooey,*" I declared, barely remembering to add, "sir." "It all happened a long time ago. Whatever the merits of your case, at law it fails because of *laches.*"

"What the devil is *laches?*"

I explained. He was outraged.

"New York State stamps a time limit on the *truth*, Reverend? My father showed me our proofs of ownership. I *handled* the royal grant to Captain Slaughter, sir—*traced* King William's and Queen Mary's signatures with my finger—*studied* my father's copy of the All Angels lease. And before he died, he made me swear to redress your church's theft."

"Then you need merely bring your proofs to a court of law."

He broke off his very direct gaze and looked out across the Square.

"I have them no longer."

"Oh, I *see*."

Craning upwards, appearing to address *Diana,* he said, "Let me tell you the story, Reverend."

6.

"MY FATHER WAS a self-made man, Father Stackpole. He operated the famous Slaughter House hotel in St. Louis, and owned besides a wharf, stables and dry goods store—a main source of provender for the wagon trains that used to collect there before starting west. In 1860 he did $100,000 in business.

"But the Civil War came. He enlisted in the Union Army, was elected a captain of his regiment, and fought throughout Missouri and Tennessee. At Chickamauga he was directing fire against a screen of trees when an iron ball made a bloody hole in his lines before the cannon's roar even sounded.

"'*Follow me!*' he yelled, and ran like the devil for that cannon—and *took* it, by gum! Turned that gun around and began shooting up Johnny Reb with his own cannonballs!"

I nodded. My grandfather furnished a substitute, of course, his Hartford law practice being new and in want of nurture.

"Well, one day he was on patrol when rebels captured him. They dragged him to Camp Asylum in South Carolina and kept him prisoner in the open air over a freezing winter." The big man's voice broke. "Unlike most, he survived. But after the war he came home a living skeleton, and two years later coughed out his life. I was twelve years old, sir. He left my sister and me orphans, for our mother died when my sister was born. We were left to the guardianship of my father's *dear* friend, Mr. Waddell, his estate to be held in trust for us until I turned 21. My father died repeating to his *dear* friend his injunction that we be educated.

"I never trusted Waddell. He vindicated my judgment. He sent my sister Ellie, ten years old, into service—sold her off to work as a housemaid. This city boy he apprenticed to a farmer. For nine long years, I took it. The day I turned 21 I went to St. Louis—only to find that Waddell had sold out and decamped long before, and no trust containing my father's property any longer existed. Waddell stole *everything,* even the documents I handled as a child—the royal grant, the lease, *everything.*"

"Very sad, Mr. Slaughter," I said. "Did you never go to law?"

"I did, sir. I located Waddell in Denver, Colorado—living there in considerable state—and sued him, but in court he produced documents—*false* documents, rank *forgeries*—that purported to describe a debt from my father to him comprising more than the value of my father's estate.

"You see, Father, I've been cheated in the past. I'll not be cheated again." His face hardening, his gaze bore into me. "Yesterday, we hurried downtown from the Pennsylvania Station to honor my ancestors' graves in the family plot near Slaughter Manor. The Manor, I knew, was pulled down long ago, but I assumed our cemetery would be sacrosanct. What I found, sir, was no hallowed ground, but a steel *monstrosity —*"

"The Singer Building," I put in complacently.

"Surely in digging the foundations they turned up the bones of my people? Not to mention their tombstones, which might even be considered *evidence?*"

"Surely *not*, Mr. Slaughter," I said. "And to repeat myself, there's no question of your lawsuit prevailing. It will fail, not because my church is *'in cahoots'* with the courts, but because you lack *evidence*. Persisting will cost you a great deal of money and expose you to ridicule and disgrace. That's what I came here to tell you, sir."

"I am a substantial man, Father," the farmer said tersely, coming to his feet. "It's taken the sweat of 35 years, but I own about the six richest sections of land on the bend of the Arkansas River. I may not be a Vanderbilt, but I am — substantial. My wife's dead, and since my son was killed in the Spanish War, I have only my daughter. I'm prepared to spend my last dollar pursuing this matter."

"You say you'll not be cheated, sir, but in fact this sharper Weis has cozened you with his fairy tale," I replied, coming to my feet also. I believe he had not an inch on me. "All Angels will not give up one square inch of land, nor pay a penny of blackmail. You will lose, sir, as you deserve to lose."

My voice rang out as in church, and I hoped the Press in the next room was hearing my declaration. When a door opened I turned, St. George spearing his dragon, willing to undergo another burst of flash powder for righteousness' sake.

But it was not a reporter who entered, nor a photographer,

but a young woman—the loveliest I ever saw. Her hair was long and blonde, her eyes a striking cornflower blue, her lips pink and full. My loins tingled as I laid eyes on her. Tingled rather urgently.

She hurried to Slaughter. Obviously this was his daughter.

Her entrance rent the garments of my false position and stripped me of my pretensions. I stood naked and embarrassed. My bullying words were not my own, my contempt borrowed. Hiding behind the collar of my profession was the Vestry's stooge, spouting its lines and ignoring its possible—*probable?*—moral obligation to the father and daughter standing in front of me. I was play-acting.

She shot me a severe look before asking, "Dad, are you all right?"

I must have blushed beet-red. Unmoved by the man's sincerity, I was undone by a glance from the girl.

"Fine, dear, fine. Our discussion perhaps grew heated. Delia, my dear, this is Father Stackpole from All Angels. My daughter."

"Delighted—" I began.

"Father Stackpole, how *dare* you upset my father!"

"I'm sorry, Miss Slaughter, but—"

"Come away, Dad, Mr. Weis is here."

"Weis!" said Slaughter, restored to good humor.

Another door opened and a slight, large-headed figure bearing a manila envelope slithered into the room. I should have heard the hiss of the serpent as he entered, but I did not. No one thought to introduce us, but I apprehended that this negligible person was Richard Weis. Beneath his dark curls was a face I thought girlish, but which I learned in due course others thought romantically handsome (Miss Slaughter herself told me so!). Peculiarly light-colored eyes made his expression impossible to read.

"Good *evening,* Father," Miss Slaughter said.

"Miss Slaughter, Mr. Slaughter, I hope—"

"*Out,* sir!" she said.

"One moment, Delia," said Weis in the voice of a bigger man. He handed me his envelope. His eyes flashing as I took it, he stepped back quickly. "You are served with our lawsuit, Mr. Stackpole."

How it burned, that package! What a fool I felt!

"Thank you, Mr. Weis," I said, so clumsily that Miss Slaughter muffled her laughter in her hands.

I retrieved my coat and, making no remarks to the Press, walked out.

7.

BREATHLESS AND DISORIENTED, I stood on 23rd Street a minute, breathing the cold night air and admiring the Flatiron Building, before turning towards the subway. Bulbs outlined the marquees of the Great White Way of that era. Leering at me, the barker of a doubtful emporium smacked his lips and said, "I know what *you* want, Sonny boy, and we *got* it!"

All was quiet when I got back to the rectory. Sitting down at the kitchen table's oilcloth, I opened Weis's envelope, to find inside a one-page summons and a 20-page complaint.

I snacked while reading them, Mrs. Brown having left a plate for me beneath a dampened towel in her range (in the event, apparently Father Andrews had finished the bread pudding).

The summons bade Father Day, as rector of defendant All Angels Church, to present himself at District Court on such-and-such a date to answer the charges contained in the complaint.

The complaint filled out *The World*'s account in setting forth Slaughter's case, less with documentary evidence—of which there was a decided lack—than by setting forth Slaughter family tradition about their farm and the lease granted to All Angels. However unsupported, the story hung together and seemed credible, and I found that I believed it. I believed *him*. The man's sincerity was obvious.

Leaving the package on the rector's desk, I indulged in a hot shower. Afterwards, as I flapped down the hallway in robe and slippers, Father Day called me into his bedroom. He was preparing for bed.

"What news on the Rialto, Albert?" he asked as he disrobed.

"I went up to scare that farmer, Father, but I'm sorry to say I failed to do so, and they served me with their lawsuit. It's on your desk."

He laughed. "Have a boy take it over to Seyforth first thing, won't you?"

"I'll take it myself."

"Good."

"I read the complaint," I ventured.

"Oh? What do you think?"

"Despite little in the way of evidence, Father, it presents a plausible and sympathetic story. And Mr. Slaughter himself gives every appearance of probity."

He snorted.

"Father Day, I'm sorry to say I believe his story, and I think a jury might well believe it, too."

Standing in front of me unconscious of his nudity, he scratched himself thoughtfully.

"That is the way with the boldest impostures, Albert: A plausible story's concocted in hopes the gullible will swallow it. As generally they will, for when most men don't find in life the success they wish for, naturally they enjoy seeing those better blessed—as *we* are—threatened with loss. We cannot count on public sympathy in this matter. We must, as ever, rely on the rule of law."

"One thing in the complaint did amuse me," I told him. "It suggests we rename the church 'All *Angles*,' because in hanging on to what's not ours we don't miss any of them."

"I take it as a compliment," Father Day said, brushing hair off my brow. "Besides, 'All Angles' wouldn't be incorrect."

"Father?"

He massaged my bicep. "Remember St. Gregory's mission to Britain? Seeing the beauty of its fair-haired men, he exclaimed, 'But they must be angels!' And to this day they're called Angles." He rubbed the small of my back. "*Your* golden locks are purest Angle, Albert. In fact, so truly *angelic* is your beauty, I feel moved to kneel in worship—"

"Father *Day!*"

Disengaging myself, and retying the belt of my robe, I hastily bade him goodnight.

8.

NEXT MORNING I BROUGHT to the breakfast table an armload of broadsheets and tabloids. We read them with disgust. The photograph of my refusing Slaughter's hand embarrassed me—I saw the young prig again ascendant—but my fellows had fun mocking the *Pretender*, as they styled him.

The World may have scooped its rivals in reporting the arrival of *The Man Who Owns New York,* but every newspaper in town battled to find new information and heap more obloquy on our heads (popular support clearly went to the Slaughters).

I was glad of my lawyer's errand. Clutching Weiss's envelope, I shouldered through the reporters crowding the stoop.

"Anything new today, Father?" Hopkins called.

"You'll be the first to know," I returned, thinking a show of affability would not come amiss. "I'll meet with you gentlemen at 11:00 o'clock."

I walked away with a feeling of release. It was a brisk day, cloudy with cold patches of blue in the sky. A salt breeze whipping up Broadway expunged the grassy smell of horse manure. The city felt clean.

I tramped across to the offices, on Maiden Lane, of Sullivan & Cromwell, walking amidst the going-to-work traffic, the amazing army of men on the move in morning Manhattan. Downtown flowed the rush of vehicles, horses steadily pacing, streetcars gliding, elevated trains steaming, a very few motors skittering with the unlikely motions of large bugs. Men in greatcoats strode proprietarily down Broadway, while more poured out from every subway. Individuals might be sleepy or slow, but the mass spectacle represented astonishing energies.

Shrouded in the kind of privacy that crowded streets

afford, I thought about Delia Slaughter, entertaining her image with an immediacy that would have felt improper inside Father Day's bachelor establishment. She set my blood aflame. Women didn't usually mean so much to me. My ideal had ever been the fellowship of Christ and his disciples. Marriage an abstract, future concern, it was boy chums at school and college with whom I passed my time. But Delia Slaughter stepped out of the parade of passing womanhood with a quality, an allure, entirely personal.

I wanted to see her again, alone. Only *alone* could I dare — my train of thought jumped the tracks as the fingers of a lady keeping pace with me brushed against mine. Their heat jolted me.

"Want some, Handsome?" she asked, as if offering to pass the biscuits. "Want some?"

"No, thank you," I answered severely. She abruptly turned around and sped up to a man going the other way. I fingered my collar as though it choked me.

This was my first visit to Sullivan & Cromwell, a firm then in its infancy but already prosperous and influential. I was permitted to wait beneath a large crimson portrait of Mr. Cromwell, who breezed past in the equally rosy flesh some time later. Across the room a glistening object affixed to the wall drew my attention. Going up to it, I beheld — according to a brass plate — the pen President Roosevelt used to sign Mr. Cromwell's pet project, the Panama Canal Bill.

Seyforth greeted me at last.

"And what can I do for you, Father?"

"I *am* sorry to interrupt you, Mr. Seyforth, but Slaughter's cohort Weis served me with this last night."

I handed over the envelope.

"Excellent," he said. "Our copy came this morning. Nothing to it, of course."

"Don't you think that, morally speaking, they may be in the right?"

"My dear Father Stackpole!" he replied, laughing. "Not only is that not for *me* to say, that's not a correct question for *any* matter that enters the courts. Courts do not decide matters of right and wrong: Courts decide the *law*."

"Cannot *justice* sway the outcome of a case?"

"I would hate to think so, Father," said Seyforth. "What a chaotic world it would be! But I'm sure we needn't worry. Especially if this matter should come up before our fellow parishioner Judge Gerard, as I believe it will, I anticipate a favorable disposition."

"Father Day has assigned this matter to me so—"

"I shall be sure to consult with you, Father. Good day."

The stock market had opened before I stepped into the street again, as was clear from its unpopulated air. The symphonic chords of the Brooklyn Bridge still lashed the sky, but crowds no longer swept across it; sidewalks that a little earlier teemed were now deserted.

As I turned down Maiden Lane I invited the image of Delia Slaughter to return to my inner eye. Father Day's image supervening, I paused to dab a smut of New York's everlasting fall of soot out of my eye.

There was irony to my embracing a religious vocation only to find myself learning the New York real-estate game at the feet of the master. Father Day rented, traded, leased out, assembled, hypothecated, mortgaged, optioned, syndicated, leased back, built, renovated, demolished and even—very occasionally—*sold*, and did it with glee. His special calling, he told me, was to wring the highest possible returns from the parish endowment. He even confided that, with Manhattan's northward migration causing All Angels' congregation to shrink in size (although not in social exclusivity), he had proposed relocating the churchyard's illustrious dead to his new Uptown Angels Cemetery, demolishing the church and raising a skyscraper on the site.

"We might manage 50 stories on our little plot, or even 60! *Think* of it! Think of the rents! The Vestry was rather shocked, I fear," he added, "but just *think* of it!"

Surely church possessions require stewardship, but was there not something excessive to Father Day's attention to that side of things? Wasn't nurturing a real-estate portfolio too abstract a way of helping people in a city of New York's crying needs?

The bells of All Angels were ringing the half-hour when I turned down Broadway again. High overhead tiny figures moved along the girders of the Singer Building. Steel clanged against steel, and sparks—*fountains* of sparks—poured down from a dozen places aloft.

Craning upwards, I chanced to see a dreadful sight: Something came off the tower with a terrifying scream, and long seconds later there was a crash behind a board fence on Liberty Street.

Shouts and a grievous caterwauling arose, while workmen scrambled and slipped down the steel. Men turned to wipe their anguished faces, and a policeman at the curb blew his whistle frantically.

"*Father!*" yelled a navvy. "Quick, over here!"

I hurried across the street.

"A man fell off the iron," he told me and, bawling, "*Priest* here, I have a *priest*," pulled me through a crowd that respectfully made way. I looked giddily up to where framework bit off cubes of the sky, then down at the mangled remains of a man—a dead man—poised in crazy embrace with a pile of steel. A pool of blood was collecting in the dirt beneath his flayed flesh. An arm, sheared off, lay near by, as white as if broken from a marble statue. My stomach rebelling, I turned away.

"There, Father." Whether the man offered comfort or direction I didn't know, but I turned back to the mess of bone and bowel. "It's Jamie McGifford."

"What am I supposed to do?" I asked.

"Extreme unction, if you please, Father," my navvy said softly. He mistook me for a Catholic priest! Rather than explain that I was Episcopalian, priest of a church lacking the sacrament he wished performed, I protested I had no chrism, no water. A man handed me a cruet of olive oil from his lunch bucket; another, a bottle of water; a third pressed a rosary into my hand.

I blessed that oil, that water. Only the year before, when I was still at seminary, Rome had revised the sacrament's emergency form. I'd looked it over idly, with the skepticism (not to say contempt) Catholic dogma draws from Episcopal seminarians, but now, miraculously, it came to mind complete.

Kneeling, I touched the rosary to Jamie McGifford's clothing and asked the Lord to take him. Reaching into the gore with holy oil on my fingertips, I made the sign of the cross on his shattered forehead, murmuring, "Through this holy unction may the Lord pardon thee for whatever sins or faults thou hast committed." Standing up, I sprinkled holy water, adding, "Rest in peace. Amen." Bowed heads came up, caps covered them again, and the living, palpably comforted, gave way to the Beekman Hospital ambulance that came clopping up. The attendants stepped off already rolling up their sleeves.

Jamie McGifford's plunge plunged *me* into an answering simplicity. As I performed his last rites, not omitting to ask God to forgive me my imposture for Jamie's sake, I felt a power new in my experience. If I play-acted the part of Roman

Catholic priest, mimed being the conduit the crowd wished God's grace to travel, it *felt* genuine—that pretended conduit thrummed with energy and solace!

Walking down Broadway, I felt sick, shaken and—God forgive me—strangely exhilarated.

9.

APPROACHING THE RECTORY, I could see the Press awaiting my promised appearance. But I had no heart to go so quickly from the spiritual to the material.

Instead I ducked around into Trinity Place, entered the rectory's tradesmen's entrance and passed into the church. There was no one there; it was hushed and sacred and beautiful. The church as rebuilt after the fire was a plain structure, thrusting upwards in simplified gothic style a steeple that in olden days was New York's tallest erection. To mark its centenary Father Day commissioned Stanford White to make gorgeous interior additions: bronze chandeliers, a walnut reredos, gilded grillwork. English saints now marched in stained-glass procession across windows made by William Morris, their rich colors splashing the faux-marble walls. (It was at the same time that White installed the rectory's men's-club opulence.)

I walked the length of the nave to the baptismal font in the vestibule. This ancient relic was my favorite feature: a shallow bowl of porphyry fully nine feet across, wheeled out of a temple at Memphis under White's supervision, shipped down the Nile and across the Atlantic and installed inside All Angels with due engineering panache. Its inner rim was carved with an *ouroboros*, a snake biting its own tail; the wet stone looked shellacked. The font always seemed illuminated from within, to reap from the surrounding shadows a ruddy light glowing with divine (if very possibly not Christian) immanence.

Its ancient pagan force somehow compelled me to consult it as an oracle.

Of course I knew that working with Father Day was a marvelous professional opportunity. It put me on the path to churchly prominence. My predecessors—New England college athletes like myself—without exception had gone on to rich suburban parishes. Such had always been my dream.

But in a world of bodies and souls at peril—of Jamie McGiffords—what matters except the Good News of Christ? And with the appearance of Delia Slaughter, I sensed where my personal happiness might lie: in performing humble parish duties in some pestilential quarter of the city, a stalwart helpmeet by my side.

Acting as the Vestry's agent, I'd antagonized Delia; but if she were worth the winning, would she not forgive what I had to do on my church's behalf? It wasn't my fault the responsibility of handling All Angels' response to her father's claim was mine.

From my pallid outline on the water's surface arose a niggling whisper: *Responsibility* was vested in me, yes, but what *authority?* So far I was chasing after events, finding myself always a step behind.

I touched a fingertip to the font's tense surface—and to my horror saw a red ribbon curl off and writhe into nothingness. There was blood on my hands.

The street door opened and glare obliterated my outline.

"Something wrong, Rover Boy?" asked a figure holding a homburg.

"Not at all, Mr. Hopkins. Just haven't started my Sunday sermon yet."

"Put 'er there, Reverend," he said, thrusting his ink-stained fingers into mine, dripping with holy water. "*My* Sunday feature's due, too."

"Perhaps we can trade jobs, Mr. Hopkins? I'll make up some story to excite people—"

"—while I preach on the rights of stolen property?"

I felt my blood rush.

"*C'mon*, Rev, this place is a whited sepulcher," Hopkins said. "You know it and I know it. All Angels is a trust up there with your Steel Trust and your Rubber Trust: the *Church* Trust. The *Soul* Trust."

"I'm sure I don't know what you mean, Mr. Hopkins."

"Then you disappoint me, Rev. You're not like the rest. You're no hard-bitten old cleric as used to the ways of the world as any roué. Day's taking advantage of that innocent phiz of yours so nothing gets in the way of his building up a church as rationalized and profitable as the Standard Oil Trust. That sit OK with you?"

I made no answer. He was hitting the mark, and he saw it, too.

"Makes me think our rube must have something," he concluded.

"Impossible that Mr. Slaughter will ever possess any of our property."

"Oh, I don't doubt *that*," said Hopkins. "The holy fix is *in*. He'll turn up dead in a ditch before *that* happens. But tell me, in a just world, would he own acreage worth a billion bucks?"

"That figure's bandied about," I replied, "but at the present day, 700 or 800 million would be a truer valuation."

Hopkins looked down at the water before he spoke. "Funny thing: We're both supposed to be in the business of speaking truth. What *happened?*"

"If you'll excuse me, Mr. Hopkins."

"Anyone going to talk to us reporters?"

"I'll be over shortly."

He left the church. Bathed in the font's radiant blush, I dabbled my fingers and took a deep breath. My exchange with Hopkins—I parroting the parish line—revolted me. The whisper came again: *Responsibility, but what authority?* Was it not arranged that I should hand out the official line, while machinations behind the scenes settled the situation? Was I not poised to fail? Poised by my own rector to accomplish nothing, save earning Delia Slaughter's contempt?

But how to find the authority I needed?

The solution came to me: I had to *assert* it—assert my authority to examine the Slaughter claim and either prove it as true or expose it as false. Nothing less positive would do. It was up to me.

And surely an honest result—whatever it was—would neutralize Delia's disdain? Surely she wasn't invested in the dream of riches to the extent her father was? I sensed that hers was a personality better pleased managing a farmyard than by gaining entrée even to Mrs. Astor's ballroom.

But *how* to do it? The archives—despite Father Day's scoffing—beckoned as the likeliest receptacle of proof. Yet I might look there in earnest and miss the crucial evidence, or search in vain for documents that either never existed or had been burned or otherwise extirpated long ago. But finding proof either for or against Slaughter's claim was the only way I could exert power over my own fate, so that was what I would try to do.

Letting out a great breath, feeling more at peace, I crossed into the rectory ready to address the Press, though leaving it to the moment to know what to say.

I was just in time to see Father Day pushing the last reporter out onto the steps.

"—I *repeat*, should Mr. Slaughter persist with his frivolous action, we shall counter-sue for slander," he was saying. "That's it for today, gentlemen. Good *morning*.

"Ah, Albert, there you are: I took care of them for you."

10.

"A WORD, FATHER DAY?"

"Certainly, Albert."

I lowered my voice, that the maids might not overhear. "Father, you gave me responsibility for the Slaughter matter, but I find I lack authority—"

"Goodness *no*, Albert! By no means! Your authority comes straight from *me*. I had no idea you were in any doubt over it!"

"Well, on that basis, then, Father."

"What other basis could there be? Do just as you see fit, short of absolutely settling the matter—the Vestry will have the final word, of course. Albert, if ever you have concerns, I wish you'd come to me! My door's open 24 hours a day."

"Thank you, Father. Incidentally, I do mean to undertake the search of the archives I spoke of. It's the only way to put all doubts to rest."

"As you see fit. Do not rush yourself. Father Morris has taken to your old duties with relish."

I returned to the church, opened a door in the sacristy and descended the creaking steps to the arena of my future labors.

All Angels' archives occupied the church's crypt, which I'd previously seen only on my introductory tour some weeks earlier. It was a dank, dark space smelling of mildew, with a stone floor and whitewashed rock walls. Bare bulbs dimly disclosed the disheartening sight of shelves and bookcases bulging with papers, tables piled high with crammed letter-files, stacks of papers receding into the shadows to every side and obscuring the few tombs and monuments. Father Day boasted that the church hadn't discarded a single document since the fire (of course, he saw to it that current records were kept in impeccable order in the offices upstairs). Paper, paper, everywhere.

I jumped when Mr. Gamble, the elderly deacon who served as archivist, woke up from a stool-top nap.

Explaining my mission, I said I wished to find Queen Anne's grant, plus any title deeds to All Angels' demesne.

He picked at the fabric of his smock. Knees akimbo, lower lip thrust out, he looked like a schoolboy being punished. "The archives are in some confusion, Father Stackpole," he told the floor. "So were they before I came, and so will they be after I'm gone."

"Well, where will I find the earliest deeds, Mr. Gamble?"

"Oh dear, nothing of that nature down *here*, I assure you."

"Perhaps I'll just poke around," I murmured.

I pulled open a drawer of the nearest cabinet and took out a handful of papers. The first piece I strained in that light to make out recorded an 1871 baptism. Behind that was a receipt dated 1896 for repair of a drainpipe, then a program for

Advent services of, it appeared, 1828.

"Mr. Gamble, perhaps you can instruct me on the principle followed in organizing these papers?"

"Oh, my predecessor, Mr. Stephens, did that," he responded. "He was in his second childhood when they put him down here, you know. Spent five years shuffling everything, and if he did it according to any principle, that principle escapes *me*. Made a dreadful mess, Father! *Dreadful!*"

"So you — ?"

"*I* put like with like." Brightening, he gestured in front of himself. "Like with like."

I took a look at the stack he indicated, the one that had pillowed his head. By "like with like" he apparently meant putting together papers of similar size. His stack, made up of pages about seven inches by nine, included Sunday bulletins from the year previous, a parishioner's letter dated 1810 and an undated charity flyer. The pile next to it included printed hymns and an 1892 calendar.

Remonstrating with the old man would be no use. Foreseeing that my sojourn in the archives would not be brief, I returned upstairs and had our porters carry down from the parish house two desks, two chairs, two desk lamps and a rug.

Thus made more comfortable, Mr. Gamble resumed work, his "sorting" now confined to stacks first vetted by myself, and I plunged into the depths for the rest of the afternoon, blacking my hands in leafing through thousands of sheets — getting through but a minute fraction of the whole. It was not unpleasant work, however, for Delia's face rose up in front of me and accompanied me in a ghostly, complaisant way.

But so far as the object of my search was concerned, I turned up nothing save a shrewd suspicion that, however assiduous my efforts, nothing bearing on Slaughter's claim would surface. My best hope of countering what Hopkins called "the holy fix" was in all likelihood a charade.

Later, after sluicing my very nostrils clear of grime, I bolted dinner while my fellows made their jokes about the *Pretender*. Then, bundled up against the wind, I descended to the I.R.T. A train roared up the tunnel with portentous hums and flashes, squealed to a stop and bore me through a flickering forest of pillars. I was determined to see Delia Slaughter and try to repair the damage of our first meeting.

All day, it had been growing on me that I was in love with her.

11.

TONIGHT A BESIEGING ARMY pressed at the doors of the Prince of Wales suite. Weis was acting as major domo. Men crowded up and stated propositions from behind their hands, women carrying sick children whispered requests, and to each he nodded either yea or nay—rather, invariably *nay*—and had them escorted to the elevators. But through this throng Weis admitted me instantly. His hand was the coldest I ever touched.

The reception room was also crowded. A waiter handed me a flute of champagne as I looked for the Slaughters. This evening there was no one from the Press.

Slaughter I found at the side, bending into the coiffure of a siren of 40. Seeing me, he straightened up in some confusion, but greeted me kindly. His message I took to be, "Yes, Father Stackpole, we find ourselves on opposite sides, but we respect each other, and no mere legal question shall be suffered to interfere with *that*." In so gentlemanly a way did he adhere to this unspoken pledge throughout my courtship of his daughter that we remained the best of friends. He also introduced me to his bewitching partner, the widowed Mrs. Vandervliet. The lady smiled expertly, her eyes glittering bright as her diamond necklace.

"Delia's here some place, Reverend," Slaughter remarked, and returned to his widow.

I surveyed the room—accidentally meeting Weis's gaze as I did so—and saw Delia just coming away from a group. I stuttered my apology for having upset her father the previous evening.

She interrupted with a smile.

"That's all right, Father Stackpole. We each have our role to play in this comedy. I forgive you yours."

It was more handsome than I dared hope.

"Thank you, Miss Slaughter," I said, and asked, "Are you giving a reception? The champagne's excellent."

"No, Father, you surprise us living what is apparently the ordinary home life of multi-millionaires. Visitors come and must be entertained. Please don't tell anyone I was milking cows so recently as Monday."

"Who are these people?"

"Some dined with us at Delmonico's. There you behold the Cleveland Dodges. Or are they the Morris Jesups? Father and I are conquering New York, Father Stackpole. But then, it's only natural for us of fantastic wealth to hang together. You others cannot understand us."

"We can but try," I said gallantly.

"Oh, and some, believe it or not, are long-lost cousins!

There are some very determined Slaughters here. One Henry Slaughter just arrived from Kentucky full of family feeling, though we have yet to hit on what our connection might be.

"Look on and be amused, Father. All are lighted up within with the beautiful hope of a billion dollars, or a sliver thereof, or the simple joy of proximity. Do you realize that a billion dollars unites the wealth of a *thousand* millionaires? With riches unlimited at our command, we cannot be mean with the champagne... You see how unreal it seems. I don't believe in a dollar of it as yet."

"I'm glad to hear you say that, Miss Slaughter, given the heavy odds against—"

Her eyes flashed. "You mean your odious word *laches*? Yesterday I'd never heard it, but today I'm well versed in how fraud invalidates *laches*."

"*Laches* or not, so much time has passed, there's such a dearth of records—and then this man Weis! Do you trust him?"

She blushed.

"No, I don't, Father. In fact, I feel a marked antipathy towards that gentleman."

I found myself relaxing. Unconsciously I suppose I'd feared him as a rival.

"Miss Slaughter, today I began a search for records related to the matter, and I promise not to suppress anything that could benefit your side."

"I see your collar, Father, I know whose side you're on. But let me tell you, this thing's made my father happier and more hopeful than anything since my brother died."

"I fear a fall from such a height, Miss Slaughter, especially seeing how expensive your establishment here must be."

"It's not certain that the hotel's charging us anything at all. Publicity, I'm told."

"What a strange thing."

I was delighted to find her so agreeable to talk to, but our real communication was of the senses. Her wide-set eyes and shapely lips made me want to place my mouth over hers. I don't know how I resisted the temptation.

"Isn't it?" she said. To my look of confusion, she supplied, "Strange that publicity can be worth money? Stranger still that money should be so worshipped?"

"A false god indeed. Please call me Albert. 'Father' seems especially unsuitable."

"If you call me Delia. Do you come from money, Albert? Oh, what a pretty blush!"

"From a respectable family only."

"As do I. Kansas wheat?"

"Connecticut law, and so forth. Delia, I've something serious to say."

"I thought we'd finished with that topic."

"It's not that," I faltered. "Delia, last evening, when I first saw you—"

Her eyes responded to something past me as Weis touched my shoulder. "Care to meet Mother, Mr. Stackpole?" he asked.

I turned around to find a couple regarding us from across the room. They made a striking pair—a plump woman giving me a proud and scoffing look, and a man who resembled Titian's portrait of Pope Paul III. Spindly fingers gripped the arms of his chair while his hooded eyes sized up the world for the kill. A chill passed down my spine.

"Certainly," I said, and we went over.

"Mother, this is Mr. Stackpole of All Angels Church. Mr. Stackpole, my mother."

"Charmed, madam," I said.

She nodded neutrally and advanced no hand, but the old man lifted his be-ringed fingers.

"I'm Richie's uncle, Abe Weis," he said. "We've heard about *Dick Rover*. Also I hear Richie gave you a little present last night?"

"Sir, have you a part in this chicanery?"

His face softened and he opened a hand. "What chicanery?" he asked. "I happen to be the principal of my nephew's firm, that's all."

"Mr. Weis, I'm not the principal of All Angels, but only its most junior curate. Those with whom you and your nephew must deal are tougher, more experienced men."

"Fortunate for your side," he remarked. Weis's mother giggled.

I decided to take my leave, but not before shamelessly presuming on my cloth to issue a subtle suitor's invitation to Delia. I found her cornered by Weis, with whom she was speaking with obvious signs of emotion and disgust.

"Excuse me," I said, interrupting. "Delia, Sunday morning I preach at St. Cuthbert's on Tompkins Square, and it would please me if you and your father were there."

Weis whispered something into her ear. He had to rise to his toes to reach it, so undersized was he.

"We may be busy—" she said as if by rote. She broke off and looked at me warmly, while Weis's jaw tightened. "No, Albert: We'll be there."

12.

IN THOSE DAYS I spent hours composing a sermon, writing out every word beforehand. But my work in the archives precluded preparing for that Sunday's other than trying to bear in mind my text *(John 2:13-17)* as I worked (though it failed to displace Delia's image, smiling encouragement in front of me). For the first time, I trusted to inspiration.

St. Cuthbert's was a satellite chapel to All Angels, one of several in poor neighborhoods of Manhattan. We with no regular pulpit assignments were always welcome to preach there. The handsome church towers over Tompkins Square Park, standing in painful contrast to the tenements on either side. Few of the Slavs swarming the streets were Episcopalian, I imagine, but the popularity of St. Cuthbert's Settlement House insured a certain Sunday attendance.

Before the service I peered out and saw Slaughter sitting stiffly beside Delia. Weis flanked her other side, his silver eyes shining. To my surprise, Hopkins of *The World* sat two pews behind.

Holy Eucharist at St. Cuthbert's was not so high as at All Angels, but the congregation appeared satisfied with the ritual. My moment came. I ascended to the pulpit. It felt lofty as a crow's nest.

"The Gospel according to John," I intoned—or, rather, croaked. Clearing my throat, I read:

> And Jesus went up to Jerusalem, and found in the temple those that sold oxen and sheep and doves, and the changers of money sitting: And when he had made a scourge of small cords, he drove them all out of the temple, and the sheep, and the oxen; and poured out the changers' money, and overthrew the tables; And said unto them that sold doves, Take

these things hence; make not my Father's house an house of merchandise.

"Brothers and sisters in Christ," I began, not confident that anything would follow.

But words filled me up! I spoke extempore as though a lick of flame flickered over my head!

"... Jesus elsewhere tells us to render unto Caesar what is Caesar's, render unto God what is God's. That injunction reinforces His lesson here: Do *not* let us mix God and Mammon. Let us keep our temple sacred to Him, and pure, and not desecrate it by commerce."

Before me slivers of Delia, her father, Weis and Hopkins revolved like crystalline shards in a kaleidoscope. Preaching tends to blind my outer eye in favor of my inner.

"Commerce has its place: Let us acknowledge the marvelous combinations of capital that move earth as never before, even as they besmirch the heavens with smoke and pierce them with new Towers of Babel. We reap wondrous piles of gold, but let us keep gold and the love of it and pursuit of it from contaminating *our* temple. Don't let us soil our worship of God with considerations of gain that might tempt us away from Him."

And more in that impassioned vein; alas, pure babble to that congregation. But that impromptu babble served to clarify his thinking on one issue for one person there: for *me*. It brought me face to face with a conviction I hadn't before articulated, that All Angels more closely resembled the defiled temple of John's Gospel than the church doing Christ's work I had dreamed of joining.

Finishing, I glanced at my guests. Delia looked meltingly back, Slaughter sat fierce and proud. Weis's response I couldn't read.

Afterwards, reactions differed. Father Sorrow, St. Cuthbert's pastor, shook his head, saying, "My boy, I fear for your future." Some of the more prosperous-looking congregants seemed affronted as they filed out, but shabbier types sawed off my arm with enthusiasm. Weis said he found it "interesting." Slaughter gripped my hand in both his; some emotion welling up within him made speech impossible. Delia placed warm fingers in mine, saying, "Thank you, Albert, you preached beautifully," and invited me to dine with them.

As Hopkins left he said, "Didn't know you had it in you, Rev."

13.

WITH MY SERMON I passed a test given me unawares by Weis, as emerged that evening.

Meanwhile, I cheerfully taught Sunday School next door, then, having left word at All Angels that I was dining out, traipsed up Avenue B to 14th Street, across to Broadway and up the Ladies' Mile to Madison Square.

Sundays were then, as they are still, an outdoor pageant for New Yorkers, and I found the streets filled and the lobby of the Fifth Avenue Hotel deserted. Upstairs the Prince of Wales suite seemed empty indeed; there was only Slaughter, his lady friend Mrs. Vandervliet, Delia, the inevitable Weis and his apparently equally inevitable mama.

We ate our dinner overlooking the Square, served by

waiters who brought up the meal in covered dishes, and no word about the lawsuit was spoken. Instead we discussed the frosty weather and the prices of wheat and AT&T stock (Slaughter, it developed, for years had been plowing his farm profits into shares of Telephone, and now was engaged in selling some of his "engravings" — as he humorously referred to the stock certificates — to defray the expenses of his New York stay and the lawsuit. Mrs. Weis and Mrs. Vandervliet spoke in hushed tones exclusively to each other, breaking off whenever anyone turned to them.

The meal ended as the sun, quiescent all day, suddenly flashed gold into Madison Square, superfluously gilding *Diana* before fading into darkness as the Garden blinked on its nighttime raiment, dotting its walls and tower in Moorish motifs. Bells near by rang for evening prayer.

Slaughter was in an expansive mood, over brandy regaling us with tales of Kansas. I hoped Weis would go away, but although he finally escorted his mother and Mrs. Vandervliet out, both ladies were (like himself) also living at the Fifth Avenue Hotel (doubtless at Slaughter's expense) and he soon reappeared. His constant presence was a fact of life.

Eventually, in a state of happy abstraction, Slaughter pushed his snifter away. Realizing it was time to put him to bed, Delia rang for his valet and helped him to his room. Weis and I should have taken our leave beforehand, but we couldn't very well depart in her absence.

There was chilly silence between us, until Weis broke it. Weighing his glass, he said, "Not to revert to forbidden topics, Mr. Stackpole — "

"There are no such topics, Mr. Weis. Please feel free to say whatever's on your mind."

"Very well. I have something to show you, if you care to see it."

"Certainly."

For a disconcerting moment he continued to regard me through the distorting bulb of his snifter. It made his face hideous. Then he drained its dregs, put it down and stood up.

"In here," he said, unlocking a door and taking me where I hadn't been before, into a windowless room provided with desk and bureau.

To my alarm, he locked us in. Unlocking the bureau he tenderly withdrew a leather portfolio and placed it atop the desk. Undoing the clasps, he opened it to reveal an aged parchment with a singed right edge, adjusted the lamp and motioned me close.

Bending low, I read what appeared to be the language of a lease, including the legal description of a tract expressed in metes and bounds, engrossed in flowing old-fashioned script, with *f* for *s*:

> ... *comprifing two hundred* Acres, *more or less, the whole of the* Flaughter Farm *given by* Royal Grant, *to be leafed by* All Angels Church *for a* Period *of ten* Years *from the* Date *firft written above...*

That date was March 31, 1783. At the bottom were the signatures of Daniel Slaughter and Philip Rutherford, then rector of All Angels.

My breath stopped! Here was the missing lease, proof that would strip the church of its holdings and bring Slaughter his inheritance — make him richer than Rockefeller!

"Good Lord!"

"This scrap, you see, proves Mr. Slaughter's story," Weis remarked. "Probably it's the sole extant copy of the lease in question. You know the tale of Waddell's theft? He stole this, among other items not yet recovered."

"*Extraordinary!* Why have you not shown this before?"

"In due course, Mr. Stackpole. The rules of court decree that your side be told of it. But in good time. So much of legal process, I understand, is a matter of tactics. And it will, you must admit, scarcely be believed. They will accuse Mr. Slaughter of forgery."

That filthy scrap glowed as my hand hesitated over it. Weis was quite right, of course.

"Go ahead, Mr. Stackpole, rumple it the more. It's lasted this century and a quarter. You see I trust you. But I hope this doesn't place you in a difficult position."

"I am my own man, Mr. Weis."

Thus do tempters work. I caressed the proof positive of the truth of Slaughter family legends.

"This document, Mr. Weis," I managed to whisper. "Would it not be more *useful*... even *dispositive*, as the lawyers say, were it to be found in the church archives? No one then could accuse Mr. Slaughter."

"That is where it belongs," he said.

I touched it again, breathed in its acrid, organic odor, and turned my head to find Weis's smooth, fine-grained face next to mine, his eyes flicking along the old calligraphy and his breath falling sweetly upon me. The rumble of New York, subdued on a Sunday night but never entirely suppressed, seemed to build to a crescendo as I drank in that old document and the astonishing powers it contained.

I straightened up and stepped backwards.

"I— You—"

"Yes, Mr. Stackpole?"

"It won't *do*, Mr. Weis. I couldn't possibly *introduce* anything into the archives—*especially*— No, *never*."

He closed the portfolio and clasped it shut.

"I merely wished you to see."

Saying nothing more he put it away and unlocked the door.

I took my leave, agitated and confused. It's not flattering to be taken for a kind of sneak thief.

14.

THOUGH IT WOULD NOT be accurate to call that period the *happiest* of my life, no other has been so chock-full of *pleasures*. Futile mornings spent grubbing through the crypt were followed by resplendent afternoons and evenings courting the greatest heiress in the land. (My hours in the archives I limited, both from concern for my eyesight and from a juvenile species of pique after Father Day refused my request for more hands to examine the papers. "We're stretched as it is," he told me. "You know that. It is our perpetual condition." So much for my supposed authority!)

But it seemed Father Day considered my companionship with Delia of service to the church. He joked once that I was keeping it "all in the family." Denton Slaughter also seemed to approve.

Delia was curious about New York, and excited by it, so we made daily explorations, always incognito. Shucking my collar and topping her with the kind of hats favored by shop assistants rendered us unrecognizable save as a handsome young couple. Slipping out her hotel's back door onto 24th

Street, we pioneered routes along the flower shops of Seventh Avenue or fruit markets of Ninth, or strolled the Fifth Avenue or the Ladies' Mile.

People seemed to enjoy the sight of us together. However disguised we were—and I felt it prudent to acquire a blond mustache that adhered to my upper lip by means of paste (only once did it drop off, into a dish of ice cream we were sharing; Delia promptly stuck it over *her* lip)—those walks acknowledged to the world what we were to each other. We never spoke of emotions, but our looks and glances expressed them. I came to feel the near-avowal of my love on only the second evening of our acquaintance a mistake, that Weis's interruption had been fortunate; taste demanded that I wait to speak until the lawsuit's end, however hard it was to endure the delay, however congested with longing my veins and limbs.

We visited the Metropolitan Museum and the Museum of Natural History, toured City Hall, rode the ferry to Staten Island, climbed Miss Liberty's torch, paid our respects at Grant's Tomb. We saw our first moving pictures in a 14th Street storefront, duly dodging, terrified, out of the way of the screen's onrushing locomotive.

And we attended the opera. Our first was Bizet's *Carmen* at the Academy of Music. In that musical projection of emotion we could savor our own turbulent new feelings. Soon we were attending two or three performances a week, by preference at the new Metropolitan Opera House on Broadway at 37th Street; whereas the old Academy of Music was constructed for the display of its patrons, the Met offered greater discretion. In fact, we liked best its standing room, private posts behind the seventh level of seats, refuge of students and the poor. With us, the joke of the greatest heiress preferring the cheapest tickets never staled.

Of course Delia had a social life in which I had no part. At her father's behest she accepted invitations from the daughters of prominent families to Tuxedo, Pocantico and Great Neck, where she smarted under a barrage of hints meant to give her manners a New York polish. She returned having had no difficulty in seeing through the motives of her hostesses or of the bachelors they introduced.

"It's Father's *claim* they like so well," she told me. "If we win the claim, I shall have sisters and brothers aplenty — with *husbands* to spare! But it's *contingent*."

The Met that winter performed Wagner's *Ring* cycle. Even today I cannot hear *The Ride of the Valkyries* without being taken back to seeing the parti-colored reflections from stage lights playing over Delia's face, music crashing upon us and dying out on the wall behind.

One evening, grateful for the privacy at our end of standing-room's semi-circular brass rail, we watched a fiery young conductor named Toscanini conduct Johanna Gadski singing Brünnhilde in *Die Götterdämmerung*. In the last act, I espied Father Day standing directly across from us, at the rail's opposite end. Through Delia's opera glasses I saw him in close converse with his neighbor, a young, Italian-looking mechanic, as he appeared to be. Like me, Father Day had discarded his clerical collar; in fact, he adopted what seemed formal garb for such cheap heights: white tie and a cutaway coat.

As the music swelled and Brünnhilde advanced to fire Siegfried's funeral pyre, I saw Father Day grip the rail with both hands and the mechanic take his place behind him. Bracing himself with a stiff arm, the young man spat in his other hand and did something out of sight that made both faces shudder. Then that hand grabbed the rail, too, both his flanking Father Day's.

Throughout the scene, while Brünnhilde sang *"Rest Thee!*

Rest Thee! Oh God!" before mounting her horse and urging it blissfully into the pyre, the Italian's features contorted as if he were effortlessly at work, and Father Day's head jerked, at first in time to the music, then rapidly, spasmodically. This strange sight was shielded from the other standees by the divisions along the rail's curve; of the thousands in the house, I believe I alone saw them. At the music's climax, agony seized their features and Father Day's mouth opened in a (presumably) silent scream. Then convulsions were at an end; the rapture of exquisite release suffused their faces.

Whispering to Delia that I would return in a moment, I stepped behind, went around and came up behind them. The Italian sensed my presence, for he turned and—if, in the riot of fire-red bouncing off the stage, I read his expression aright—*grinned,* and lifted the tails of Father Day's cutaway to reveal split trousers and glimpses of fleshy moons.

Shocked, sick to my stomach, I staggered back to Delia's side. When I spirited her out she was concerned to find me sweating in the chill night air.

My shaking gradually abated. Not so the tremor of my thoughts, after finding *abomination* at the heart of All Angels!

As I saw Delia home, I was weighing my choices. They were stark: Acceding to disorder and hypocrisy, I could go on as before. Or—if that course happened not to suit my conscience—I could use such power as lay to hand.

By the time we reached her hotel, my mind was made up. I would use Weis's lever. I would place that old parchment lease where it belonged—in All Angels' archives—and thereby deprive hypocrisy of its wrongful gains and restore them to their rightful owner. My doing so would be in accord with the principles of justice and the Good News of Christ.

Delia and I found her father in the reception room conferring with Weis about the roll of collateral heirs he was bedeviling himself to compile. Soon Delia went to bed, as did Slaughter, who disliked late hours but always waited up for her. In saying goodnight, he urged Weis and me to enjoy his brandy.

Weis gave me a dash of it and, gathering up the papers they'd been discussing, got up to return them to the little side room.

As he restored them to the bureau, I stood in the doorway — *loomed*, rather.

"Yes, Mr. Stackpole?"

"The other evening..."

I dwindled into silence, uncertain how to proceed.

But there was no need. Giving me a searching look, Weis drew me in, locked the door and took out from the bureau the portfolio he'd shown me before.

"Yes," I said softly.

"Very good," he said, holding it out.

Unceremoniously, I grabbed it and stuffed it in my armpit. Easy as that. Curtly I nodded goodnight, and carried my booty out of there.

A doorman installed me in a hansom cab. As we trotted downtown I lived a veritable suspension of time. Conscience compelled me to do what I was doing, but sitting there hugging my treasure I felt distinctly criminal.

I had the cabbie take me to the tradesmen's entrance on Trinity Place, where I dismissed him and waited in the shadows until the horse had clopped away and I was certain no one was about. I was chary of being seen to enter the rectory with what I was carrying.

As I brought out my key, Mrs. Brown's tabby scampered up and rubbed my legs. I crept inside, the portfolio pinned to my side, and Rex dashed into the kitchen.

"Why, *kitty*," I heard Mrs. Brown say. "Where did *you*

come from? Are you hungry?"

She filled a bowl for him, to his gratified mewing, while with infinite care I stole to the door that communicated with the church proper, closed it behind me, opened the door to the crypt, flicked on the lights and crept downstairs.

Amidst the mildew I was considering where to hide the lease when I began to hear noises. Mice nibbling? Ghosts stirring? Or merely a train rumbling up its tunnel? Shoving the lease in an ancient ledgerbook, only its scorched edge poking out, I got out of there.

The empty portfolio I placed in an ashcan reeking of fish several doors down Trinity Place, and quietly returned indoors, tiptoed upstairs past Father Day's room; and thus to bed, with the beating heart of an anarchist who has planted his time bomb.

Father Day came down to breakfast humming.

"Wagner?" I hazarded.

"Why, yes, Albert: *Love's Greeting*. Saw *Götterdämmerung* at the Met last night."

"We were there, too. How did you like it?"

"Delectable, altogether *delectable*."

"Did you go by yourself?" I asked.

He tilted his head, registering that it was an odd question.

"I did *go* by myself, but as it happened—though you needn't say anything, silent charity being so dear to Our Lord's heart—I happened to meet a young lover of opera who lacked the wherewithal to buy a ticket, and paid his entry."

"Oh!"

"The greatest pleasure, Albert, is to give pleasure. Ah: sausages. *Delectable*, Mrs. Brown, *delectable!*"

15.

MOTION AND COUNTER-MOTION were filed, deadlines set and enlarged, hearings scheduled and postponed. In other words, the law took its majestic course with regard to *Slaughter versus All Angels Church*.

My bomb ticked away as Christmas came and went. It was not yet time to set it off, and on both sides the affair took on a grind and tension. Father Day, outwardly confident as ever, yet found difficulties forming a syndicate to construct an office block on Chambers Street; even the Vestrymen, usually eager to come in on his deals, hung back. "'Wait until the Slaughter claim's settled,' they tell me," he complained. "Don't they realize, it *is* settled?"

But poor Slaughter had it worse, so burdened with anxieties, so taxed with grandiose fantasies, that he aged ten years in two months.

Given their astronomical New York expenses, funds were becoming more and more a concern. Although the Fifth Avenue Hotel withheld its bill, Slaughter knew that the lion of the season must present a costly front. Thus his carriage and matched pair, driver and postilion for the daily round of Central Park; in addition, his valet, his secretary, plus whatever Mrs. Vandervliet was able to extract. Adorning Delia as became her station required seamstresses and a lady's maid, of course, as well as jaunts to Tiffany's.

In addition, every mail brought begging letters that ranged from heart-rending pleas to brusque and detailed demands; the good man read every one and probably, despite denials, disbursed quiet gifts in advance of his own inheritance. And far the biggest share, I'm sure, went to Weis and the expensive law firm he engaged to do battle with Sullivan & Cromwell.

Accordingly, Mr. Slaughter's "engravings" continued going to market. Fortunately, the price of Telephone was among the stock market's firmer offerings during that unsettled time following the Panic of 1907. But his expenses finally eating through the last of his "engravings," he began to sell, one at a time, his farms. Delia opposed this. She proposed instead a drastic reduction in state—dismissing the carriage and staff, renting a flat, refusing invitations. But her father would have none of it, and the acres began to go. Nothing on earth—*nothing*—can withstand the expense of a New York lawsuit.

Slaughter privately confided to me that he might soon be under the necessity of borrowing. He insisted he was easy in his mind at the prospect, that any advance would represent but the minutest fraction of his expectations, and that he was assured his credit was unlimited, both by the bankers he hobnobbed with and the moneylenders who, following what scent I know not, began crowding up. But the tremor in his voice betrayed his unease.

I hated to see my friends suffer when at any moment I could put an end to their misery, but the time was not yet ripe. Therefore, I slogged on in the archives, even began to find the miscellaneous records fascinating and the task of putting them into some sort of order congenial—at least more so than returning to the desk outside Father Day's door. And always while I worked, Delia's image swam encouragingly in front of me.

In early January, she proposed to her Father that they make a trip South. To her surprise and pleasure, he agreed. Despite their importunities, even stronger on his part than hers, I declined to accompany them; it would not look well. Unfortunately, Slaughter wanting a companion (in addition to

Mrs. Vandervliet, I mean), Weis *did* go along. Delia swallowed her distaste.

Thus, as snow and ice descended on the city, they embarked aboard the private railroad car Mr. George Gould generously put at their disposal.

Delia kept me almost as well apprised of their experiences as I could have wished. They stopped at Washington, where both Kansas Senators gave them a dinner at which President Roosevelt made an appearance, but their first stay of any length was at Richmond. They made a longer one at Charleston, then paused at Jeckyll Island before sweeping south to the Breakers Hotel in Palm Beach.

In vivid contrast to New York—ever eager to suck up anyone's last dime—the South declared their money to be no good, in the delightful sense that no one would accept payment for anything. Hotel suites came courtesy of the management, locomotives pulled Mr. Gould's car *gratis*, restaurants vied to banquet them and millionaires loaned houses and staffs. There was nothing no one wouldn't do for the prospectively richest man in the land, and although the New York press had ceased chronicling their daily activities, the clippings Delia sent showed how the "sleeping-car states" (I borrow Mr. Irving S. Cobb's phrase) greeted them as royal figures.

The Slaughters still in the South, Father Day one afternoon pulled me upstairs and sat me down in front of his desk. Behind him, lent poetry by stained glass, was the daily riot of Wall Street's going home, an affair almost as competitive and jostling as the trading floor itself.

"When I assigned the Slaughter matter to you, Albert," Father Day began, an edge to his voice, "I never envisaged your spending the winter underground, sifting the accumulated trash of a century."

"If there lurks anything that can compromise our church's hold on its property, better to get it out into the open," I explained sententiously. "For such things have a way of turning up."

"Oh, undoubtedly," he replied, "if not in the first 120 years. Albert, you know it's unthinkable that we lose this lawsuit—"

"Is it so crucial, Father Day?"

"Father Stackpole! If we lost, the cathedral of St. John the Divine would go unroofed! Be left open to the elements, a ruin and monument to folly! All Angels would become an ordinary parish church, with a congregation made up of neighborhood porters and charwomen." For a moment I saw fear in his eyes; then security returned. "But we won't lose."

"How can you be sure?"

"I have confidence in my long-ago predecessor."

"The one who stole the Slaughter farm?"

"What is it Seyforth says about what's *probable* not being *provable?*" Father Day remarked. "I mean the one who ushered All Angels into the new republic, a man who saw how to turn certain rocky cornfields to churchly use. Why enrich a single family, when the welfare of *millions* can be improved?"

"A socialist, then?"

"Hardly that," he chuckled. "But this I know, Albert: Such a man leaves no loose string behind. Your friends will never recoup their loss. Life doesn't work that way. I'm grateful for your efforts. You've exerted yourself heroically. But you've failed to bring to light anything to disturb the status quo, and it's time to call a halt to the farce—and give you the new assignment you've earned.

"Come to the Vestry Room, I'm dying to show you."

I followed him there. He opened its door with a flourish. On the table stood the model of a beautiful gothic church. Easels to the side displayed exterior and interior renderings of the same structure.

"Albert, the Bishop wants to give you a parish of your own. It's a new one, St. Veronica's, out in Westchester. Cram and Goodhue submitted this idea for the church. I rather like it, I must say. What do *you* think?"

Tears started to my eyes. I suppose the model was made of painted cardboard, the elevations merely watercolor, but I believed in their limestone. There, amidst a setting of suburban luxury, was *everything* that, until a few months previous, I'd ever wanted: the bell tower rearing into a sky of dramatically composed clouds; the interior rhythm of piers and vaults that soothed and inspired; the welcoming portal.

"Father, I don't know what to say."

"Say yes. You'll do very well for Westchester—young families and the like, more your line than what we do here. Just say yes."

"After the Slaughter matter's settled, of *course*—"

"The Bishop cannot wait that long," Father Day said blandly. "Only forget about your *Rightful Heir*, and this is yours."

I swallowed, sorely tempted. "I don't know that I can, Father."

"His case will continue to its destined end, Albert, whatever that may be. Step out of it, and—"

Taking a deep breath, I tore myself away from my old dreams.

"Father Day, I must say no. Personal considerations—"

"Is it the girl?"

"I love her."

"Quite so." He turned away, flicking off the lights. "A shame. Goodhue's getting so Romish, I thought sure he'd hook you."

16.

THE SLAUGHTERS' out-of-town idyll ended on a March afternoon when Mr. Gould's car rolled to a stop in Jersey City. I met them there. Although Slaughter appeared easy and relaxed, and Mrs. Vandervliet plump and happy, the tension between Delia and Weis was electric. We ferried across the river — Weis abruptly taking his leave on the dock — and returned to the Fifth Avenue Hotel.

Slaughter looked out with interest at the new excavation across Madison Square, where machines like huge invertebrates were digging foundations for the Metropolitan Life Insurance tower, soon to supplant the still-unfinished Singer Building as tallest in the world.

He folded himself into an easy chair by a window, crossed his long legs and, sighing, sank back in bliss.

"Good to be home, Albert. I realize now the island of Manhattan *is* my home — has been, really, since before I was born."

"We've missed you, sir."

"I really begin to believe it's coming."

"What's that, sir?"

"The day your rector welcomes me to his Vestry Room. Maybe he'll be a little nervous, as I imagine Lee was at Appomattox. I'll pat him on the back, put him at ease, sit down with him and his Seyforth and the assistants. The papers will have been drawn up beforehand, I'll need do no more than glance them over, see that they transmit to me what's mine. He'll offer a pen and I'll sign my name." He blinked happily into the dusty light. "Sign my name and come into my own."

"Preserve the pen, sir, as a keepsake."

"All right, I'll save the pen. Then I'll have some settling up to do. How surprised Father Day will be when I hand him my check made out to All Angels in the amount of one million dollars! But what's a few weeks' rent? Oh yes, come settlement day, we'll be good friends, Father Day and myself."

"I don't doubt it, sir."

"And then I shall rebuild Slaughter Manor as my primary residence. I know, I know, there's a 12-story building on the site. Well, I'm knocking it down—clearing the entire block. I can afford it. And then the million, *billion* details of making things right."

Springing to his feet, he began pacing back and forth, his peace at an end.

"Above all I should like to see Delia settled." He came to a halt in front of me. "I wish she favored *you*, my boy."

Had he not eyes? I merely smiled and, putting my hand on his shoulder, together we watched the machines across the Square shoot clouds of dirt into the air. The wind brushed back the trees' new leaves, giving them a darker hue and us a pert rear view of *Diana* aiming her arrow at Brooklyn.

Delia came in then, and she and I departed for a tramp up and down the avenues, disguised as of old. It restored us to just the way we were before the Southern tour. I pressed her, but she bravely insisted that traveling with Weis "wasn't so bad."

Back at the hotel, accepting her offer of tea, I sat next to her on the sofa and almost lost control. I put my arms around her!

Fortunately she sprang away and, touching the bell pull, firmly bade me good day. Fortunate, for I don't feel I could answer for what I might otherwise have done. I returned home suffused with shame.

Even so, I knew that the moment had come for the crypt of All Angels to disgorge its secret.

It was time to explode my bomb.

17.

THAT NIGHT I stayed up reading newspapers until everybody else in the rectory had gone to bed. The headlines went to the Great White Fleet sailing around the world, but the social columns reported the Slaughters' homecoming.

When I could hear no movement, no sounds, save for faint snoring from Father Day's room, I stole downstairs, crossed into the church and descended to the crypt. There I found the ledgerbook in which was secreted the lease. Placing the ledger third from the top in the mismatched pile on Mr. Gamble's desk, the one he would "sort" first in the morning, I returned upstairs, went to bed and slept well indeed.

Next morning I lingered at the breakfast table until the doorbell sounded. Without fail, Hopkins of *The World* rang every morning at 9:00 to ask after developments. He was the only reporter to do so; the others had long since raised their siege. Mrs. Brown's curt "Nothing new" always sent him on his way.

Today I answered the door myself.

"Good morning, Mr. Hopkins," I said. "Nothing new. I'm about to spend another day searching our archives, but even I begin to doubt there's anything there."

"Mind if I poke around with you?" he asked.

My answer floored him.

"Why not?"

I took him with me over to the church and down to the crypt, where Mr. Gamble was already studying the top item on his stack, a circular advertising an Easter week choir performance of 1881.

While going through a file drawer near by, I boasted to Hopkins how we were rearranging things. But he was appalled.

"Father, pardon me for saying, but if you were serious about finding a needle in this haystack, wouldn't you get at least the Ladies Auxiliary down to help?"

"As Father Day can tell you, we are stretched as it is," I assured him.

Out of the corner of my eye, I saw Mr. Gamble pick up the next item on his pile—an 1863 bishop's letter—while I continued boring Hopkins silly with commentary on my drawer's contents. Disposing of the letter, Mr. Gamble reached for the next item—reached for the ledgerbook. He opened it. The parchment lay revealed. He brought it up to his eyes and turned it around.

The difficulty was that Mr. Gamble, his jaw having dropped, turned that parchment over and over, examined it closely and put it back in the ledger, before, distressed, taking it out again and caressing it in silent awe. This left me babbling on at length for Hopkins' benefit, and he backed up to give me the wide berth accorded madmen.

Finally Mr. Gamble spoke up. "Oh dear, oh dear, what's *this?*" he said. I ignored him. Louder, he keened, "Oh *dear,*

Father Stackpole: *Slaughter,* isn't that the name?"

"What's that, Mr. Gamble? Yes, *Slaughter.* That's the claimant. The pretender."

He pursed his lips and held the lease out at arm's length.

"Then I might have found something."

"Oh really?"

I went over, in no hurry, and plucked it from his hand. Hopkins looked over my shoulder.

"See where it says *Flaughter,* there?" Mr. Gamble's trembling finger traced the name. "Of course, the *S* resembles an *F* —"

"My goodness, Mr. Gamble!" I exclaimed. I mumbled excerpts aloud, then declared in pretended bug-eyed excitement, "It's a *lease.* Why, this might be what we've been looking for! Mr. Hopkins, look at this! Well, I *never!* I'll get Father Day."

Leaving the parchment in the reporter's hands, I ran upstairs and into the rectory, bursting past Father Morris into Father Day's office.

"Father Day! Father Day!"

"What is it, Albert? *Calm down.*"

"Mr. Gamble's found it! Just now: the Slaughter lease! Come see!"

Father Day clamped his mouth shut so tightly that bolts appeared to obtrude at the corners of his jaws. Rising up, forgetting even to lay down his pen or remove his eyeshade, he followed me to the crypt.

Hopkins had put his minutes alone to good note-taking use.

"What's *he* doing here?" Father Day demanded.

"Why, he was inquiring," I said.

"Sir, I must ask you to leave," he told Hopkins.

"Father Day," Hopkins asked, "this discovery proves

Slaughter's claim, does it not?"

"*Out!*" screamed the rector. "Get *out* of here! Get *out* of here this *instant* or I'll call the *police!*"

18.

EVEN BEFORE *THE WORLD* had its extra on the street, Seyforth arrived at Father Day's summons, along with two junior attorneys. Establishing themselves in the Vestry Room, they conferred with the rector at length. Then they dispatched Mrs. Brown to fetch me.

I went in. Seyforth sat in the Warden's chair (it swallowed him up), flanked by his colleagues. In front of him on a length of velvet reposed Mr. Gamble's discovery—the lease and, beside it, the ledgerbook (which recorded parish transactions of 1797). Me he directed to sit opposite. From the side Father Day was glancing around that handsome room as though everything in it were about to be knocked down at auction, chairs upended on a salesroom floor, windows sold to a lunchroom. He looked unhappy indeed.

Seyforth's associates interested me, for they were my doppelgängers, save that while one was fair, the other was dark. Both were big specimens with cagey faces—just what I should have turned out to be had I not heeded a higher calling. Me they ignored, chary as boys of risking contact with their disgraced fellow.

As in a play, a newsboy's soprano cry wafted up from the street: *"Extra! Extra! Slaughter lease found!"* Father Day got up and punished the casement, shutting it so hard a pane cracked.

My doppelgängers hunching their shoulders, Seyforth glared over his pince-nez the length of the table. "Father Stackpole, we wish to ask a few questions regarding this *extraordinary* discovery of yours."

"Not mine, Mr. Seyforth," I answered. "All credit goes to Mr. Gamble. *He* found the lease."

"Quite so."

His accusatory gaze redoubled by those of my doppelgängers, Seyforth inquired into the archives, their size, state and organization. His questions were minute, repetitive and exhaustive, as were my answers. At his request, I even conducted them on a tour of the crypt, Mr. Gamble gaping at us.

Back in the Vestry Room, Seyforth said severely, "I hope you realize, Father Stackpole, that the somewhat too generous rules of court — not to mention the exigencies of the newspaper publicity you were so careless as to invite — require that we share this — this *document* with the opposing side? Provide them with the very material that could cause us to lose the suit? They'll undoubtedly amend their complaint and attach this *thing* to it as their Exhibit 'A.'"

"Yes, sir," I said.

He put his hand to the velvet.

"Know, however, that before we share it I have a man who will subject it to forensic analysis." His eyes held mine as, biting off the words, he repeated, *"Forensic analysis,* Father Stackpole. He will subject it to *chemical assay,* as well as to *magnification* — even, if necessary, to *photostatic enlargement!* He will determine conclusively whether this document is authentic or a forgery."

"Good," I repeated coolly, for all that the sweat popped out on my brow. "I merely wish for the truth to be known. Like you, Mr. Seyforth."

"To be sure," he said, "but if you have anything to tell us, I urge you to speak up now, before it's too late."

"We shall ask no questions, Albert," interposed Father Day. "There will be no recriminations."

It sounds ludicrous now for me to say that I believed the lease to be genuine, but I *did*, more or less. I wanted to think it real, of course, but I knew, or thought I knew, that its prototype existed or had existed. Whether what I had secreted was the original document, retrieved from the thief Waddell, or a copy of it, or a later recreation—what Seyforth would call a forgery—never quite engaged my attention with the simplicity with which it engaged theirs.

"I have nothing to add, sir," I declared.

"Albert, as you can imagine," Father Day sighed, "this discovery means we must go through the archives with a fine-tooth comb—see what other headaches might lie in wait. We must know the worst, for we don't wish to be accused of withholding evidence."

"Quite right," I said.

"I think it best to move the archives to the parish house," he continued, "and put them in good order in fireproof surroundings."

Seyforth took it up. "Father Stackpole: You will assemble a team and complete this task, however literally Herculean it may be, in the shortest time possible." He gave me a chilly smile. "Not *quite* so bad as cleaning the Augean stables. With the entire resources of All Angels at your command, I daresay it can be done—can and *will*."

I was dismissed.

And so for an entire giddy week, while the Press had its

field day and the Slaughters braced themselves for their imminent Golconda, I was stuck first in a crypt amidst ghosts and rotting paper, then on the floor cleared for us in the parish house, driving a corps of deacons and seminarians, with the assistance of librarians from Morningside University. This great leafing through of paper, this concerted reorganization of the archives we accomplished by analyzing every piece and sorting it into its proper category in chronological order, while compiling a comprehensive and cross-referenced index. The incessant susurration of shuffled paper sounded like an army of gnawing mice.

At the end of our labors, the archives were spruce and trim and constituted, as they have ever since, a rich resource of parish and city history. To this day I take pride in having helped put them into good order.

Naturally, in those thousands upon thousands of scraps, we found nothing that shed light on the Slaughter claim or the parish's title to its land: *Nothing*. Not one shred, not one particle. *Nothing*.

19.

THE LEASE'S DISCOVERY conquered the social world's last resistance to my friends. Our great dig was still under way when they received the ultimate accolade and vindication: Mrs. Astor, unchallenged doyenne of New York Society, herself but months from expiring, invited Slaughter and his daughter to dine and dance and meet her Four Hundred.

Donning a formal black coat, my snowiest collar, I escorted Delia to the ball.

We rode uptown in a single carriage, Delia and I facing her father and Mrs. Vandervliet. Both ladies wore Worth gowns of breathtaking beauty, with the full panoply of jewels. I confess that as my fingers played with Delia's gloved ones, my excitement was such that I found it expedient to rest my top hat in my lap!

We descended at the famous porte-cochère off the Avenue (fussing with my hat, I thought desperately about the Giants baseballers) and stepped into the well-oiled workings of a great social mechanism. Doors opened and footmen shimmered forth symmetrically as in a cuckoo clock. They bowed their heads, and a hospitably simpering underbutler escorted us to the bowing butler. This personage conducted us to Mrs. Astor herself. Weighted with diamonds and supported by her granddaughters, she teetered in front of her full-length portrait as she gravely reached out to welcome Delia and her father—in full view of its Elect laying on the hands of Society, the imprimatur and blessing of her incomparable social standing.

The evening was perfect but for the snub offered by All Angels' Vestry: No Vestryman was to be seen—not one, though surely all had been invited. The Slaughters appeared not to notice, however, and I said nothing, not wishing to impair their enjoyment.

We left early, in fact shortly after our feeble hostess retired; Slaughter couldn't uproot the habits of 35 years on the farm. But it didn't matter: The blessing irretrievably bestowed, as we took our leave dowagers and debutantes alike accorded Slaughter the deep, respectful curtsies due *The Man Who*

Owned New York.

Our carriage open to the balmy evening, we trotted downtown agreeing we'd never met such nice people. And enjoyed the sight that, as it were, lighted our passage down Fifth Avenue. Slaughter, his eyes reflecting glare, bade Delia and me turn around, and we saw, several miles off, the Singer Building ablaze with lights, a lantern splashing buckets of gold into the night. After watching its construction, it was most satisfying to see the city's new beacon soar complete and finished.

"I own that," Slaughter murmured with pardonable pride. "That's *mine*."

20.

GETTING HOME, I was perplexed to find the rectory lighted up, though as I tripped up the front steps the Vestry Room windows went dark. In the hallway, I saw the backs of figures hasting out past the kitchen. Father Day, meantime, his face red and his manner flurried, detained me at the front door to demand a full account of Mrs. Astor's gala.

"Excuse me, Father," I pleaded. "A call of nature."

I hurried to the lavatory next to the kitchen. Its window, raised its usual inch, gave onto Trinity Place, where I heard voices in low converse. "Wrap it up for good and all," someone said. "Hard on the youngster, though," put in someone else. "Blot on his copybook, however stupid he is." Another voice: "But that's stupid, stupid, *stupid*."

Snapping off the light, I lowered my eye to the sill and, to my astonishment, saw Vestrymen lingering in talk as they were wont to do after their meetings.

I came out to find Father Day standing guiltily beside the staircase.

"It's late for a Vestry meeting, surely?" I asked.

"It dragged on, there were numerous items to consider."

"What went on?"

"Seyforth brought us up to date on his efforts to counter the Slaughter suit. He mentioned that Judge Gerard's been assigned to hear it—a coup for us."

"Why was I not notified of this meeting?"

"Because *I'm* still rector here!" he said with asperity. "*I* made the decision."

"But you gave me responsibility for—"

"A terrible mistake, Albert! Your handling's been disastrous! We're subjected to endless criticism in the Press, and now face a trial with no guarantee of prevailing!"

"I'm sorry, Father, I'm doing the best I can."

"You didn't have to fall in love with the girl," he wailed.

"How could I *not?*" I responded. He abruptly turned around and walked upstairs. I called after him: "Delia Slaughter's the loveliest, sweetest young woman I've ever known."

He looked over the banister. "Oh, and Seyforth wonders whether you'd please run over to his office in the morning?"

"His office?"

"At 10:00 o'clock, say, or a quarter to?"

He disappeared.

21.

I PRESENTED MYSELF promptly at the offices of Sullivan & Cromwell the next morning. My doppelgänger greeted me and, putting on his hat, crossed to a door, spoke into a room, and a moment later his fellow and Seyforth emerged, putting on their hats, also.

"This way, Father," Seyforth said, nodding at me.

And we left, a hurried little procession of four, each hauling a heavy briefcase.

"Where—?" I asked my doppelgänger.

"An emergency evidentiary hearing!"

"We telephoned Judge Gerard at home last night!" said the other.

"Good!" So I said, but my heart thumped.

We rushed a few blocks north, to the District Courthouse. On the way I happened to look down a street to find the vista of Brooklyn closed by the rusted side of a freighter gliding downriver, and felt a distinct urge to run and jump aboard. For some reason, dread filled me.

We climbed a monumental staircase to a courtroom on the second floor. Seyforth and his associates went in and settled themselves at a table up front, but me they installed in the corridor with admonitions not to stir. I sat there watching as Weis appeared, radiating confidence, and passed inside. Following him into the courtroom, looking bewildered, were the Slaughters, whom Weis directed to seats at the rear. I couldn't catch either's eye.

Through the open door I saw Weis fall into whispers with a bespectacled type whom I took to be the lawyer representing

Slaughter, one Whitehouse, whose minions flanked him at his table and occupied the bench behind. Among others who also went in were Weis's mother and uncle, and Hopkins of *The World*; how Hopkins sniffed out the hearing, I don't know.

As a bailiff bade all rise for the judge's entrance, Weis came out of the courtroom, but civilly held the door open for, of all people, Father Day and Mr. Shoatsbury as they slipped inside. Again I failed to catch either's eye. While Weis, smiling to himself, sat at a window some yards down the corridor, I admit I put my eye and ear to the crack of the doors, so saw Judge Gerard's wizened old head wagging atop his robes as he took his elevated seat and gaveled for order.

I heard him say — with a dryness that struck me as dangerous — that they were assembled to inquire into certain evidence the parties proposed to introduce in the trial of *Slaughter versus All Angels Church*. There were swift procedural exchanges I couldn't follow, and then, to my surprise and dismay, *my* name was pronounced and my doppelgänger popped up and ran out to get me.

"They're waiting!" he urged.

As in a dream — not a particularly pleasant one — I found myself standing at the front of the courtroom with my hand on the Holy Bible, swearing to tell the truth, the whole truth and nothing but the truth.

"Is it not true, Father Stackpole," Whitehouse asked, after I was seated and we had established my position at All Angels, "that your superiors ordered you to search the church archives for documents pertaining to Mr. Slaughter's claim?"

"Not quite," I replied, with the pedantic exactitude I felt was my best security. "It was *my* idea to do so. I began searching the archives on my own initiative."

"And did you find any relevant documents?"

"Personally, no, I never did."

"But did your archivist— All Angels employed an archivist named Samuel Gamble, is that not correct?"

"Yes, that is correct."

Whitehouse told the judge that the parties were stipulating that Mr. Gamble couldn't testify to his own actions, having moved to a country home for superannuated churchmen, Seyforth acknowledged the stipulation, the judge nodded and everybody's eyes came back to me.

"Father Stackpole, on the 19th of March last, did Mr. Gamble, in your presence, have greater success than you in finding a document relevant to Mr. Slaughter's lawsuit?"

"Yes, he did."

"And would you please describe to the Court exactly what Mr. Gamble found?"

"He discovered a lease, dated March 31, 1783, that assigned the Slaughter farm to All Angels Church. It was inscribed on parchment, its right edge was singed, and it was signed by both Daniel Slaughter and Rector Rutherford."

He presented the selfsame document to me, I identified it and it was duly entered into evidence.

"Now, the term of this lease wasn't 99 years or any such extended or indefinite period, was it?"

"No, sir, it specified a term of ten years."

"Meaning that it expired in 1793?"

"Yes, sir, on March 31, 1793."

"So that possession of the Slaughter farm should on that date have reverted to the Slaughter family?"

"Yes, sir—or possibly, that being a Sunday, on the next business day. I'm not sure."

"Is it, then, your opinion that this document proves that the real property held today by All Angels Church is held fraudulently?"

"In my opinion, yes," I said carefully.

"And is it your opinion that those 200 acres in fact belong to Mr. Denton Slaughter?"

"Yes, sir, that is my opinion."

I felt serene. I was speaking the truth.

Whitehouse thanked me and sat down.

"Mr. Seyforth," said the judge.

Seyforth stood up, skewering me with his eyes.

"Father Stackpole," he said, as though my name were accusation enough, "is it not true that you obtained the so-called 'lease' in evidence not from your church's archives, but from the other side in this case?"

"No!" I said. Inadvertently my voice squeaked. Clearing my throat, I repeated gruffly, "No, that is not true!"

Only then did I permit my eyes to swerve, for an instant, to Delia. She was holding the back of her hand to her open mouth in horror. Her father looked appalled.

"And, Father Stackpole, is it not true that you yourself placed the so-called 'lease' in the archives of All Angels Church—?"

"Absolutely not true!" I thundered.

"—there to repose until such time as it pleased you that it be—*ahem*—'discovered'?"

"No, no, *NO!*"

"Nothing further, Your Honor," said Seyforth, nodding at Judge Gerard.

No one would look at me. Father Day examined the floor, Shoatsbury the ceiling; the Slaughters gripped each other, whispering. I could see a sliver of Weis's face at the courtroom doors. He was failing to suppress a grin. The ends of his mouth twitched and his colorless eyes crinkled.

The judge said, "You may step down, Father Stackpole. Mr. Whitehouse, is Mr. Weis ready to testify?"

While I took a pew at the side, Whitehouse stood up and

asked to be heard in chambers.

This request, unusual as it seemed to me, was granted at once. The lawyers followed the judge out a private door; inexplicably, Shoatsbury and Father Day followed after. Even more inexplicably, Weis entered the courtroom and followed them out. We others were either told or sensed (I forget which) that this conference could take some time, so stood up, stretched, talked in normal tones.

Naturally I went over to the Slaughters. Splotches marred Delia's complexion. When I touched her shoulder, she squirmed as from the touch of a leper.

"How *dare* you, Albert!" she shot at me. "How *dare* you!"

"How dare I *what?*"

"Plant that false—"

"But Delia!"

"And then to *lie* about it!"

"Delia!"

"Lie to *me!*"

Her father pulled her away. Someone tapped my shoulder. It was Weis's uncle.

"My boy, let's talk. I fear you're not apprised of latest developments."

21.

"WHAT'S GOING ON, Mr. Weis?" I appealed. "I feel—at sea."

He sat down, patting the bench beside him. Weis's mother slid over to give me room.

"My nephew's in there confessing at this moment."

"Confessing to *what?*"

"To concocting that thing, that so-called 'lease,' and giving it to you to hide."

"But— But he'll go to jail!"

Mr. Weis smiled. "I don't think so. Don't they say confession's good for the soul? Sometimes it even helps in this world."

"*Concocting!*"

Craning around, he pointed to a mustachioed man twirling a bowler on his finger as he conversed with my doppelgänger.

"That's Seyforth's man. He's good—better than my nephew's, I guess. He examined the lease in his laboratory. It was the ink. He dissolved a little of the ink and found in it tannic acid or—I don't know *what*, but something at any rate that they never put in ink until a few years ago."

"So— So it's *fake!*" I said. "And the Slaughters—?"

"Oh, they knew nothing of it."

"So their claim—?" It was as though I couldn't think.

"Oh—their *claim*," Mr. Weis said, dropping the word like a dry twig. "That's the sad thing, their claim's undoubtedly good, but can never be proved."

"Never?"

"Not by anything that exists at All Angels, I promise you that."

I wanted to cry.

"Can I tell you a story, Father Stackpole? We have time, I think."

"Go ahead, Mr. Weis."

He crossed his legs and rested an elbow on his knee, his face lighting up with a resemblance to his handsome nephew's.

"I'm an old man now, but when I was young I wanted

adventure," he started. "Well, I left Lithuania, crossed the Atlantic, came to America. *That* was adventure. I settled in Brooklyn—that was adventure, too. But I was a farmer, what did I know from Brooklyn?

"I had a little money, so I bought a cart, a sturdy pushcart, like the ones many made their living from in those days, and loaded it with what farmers need for their animals and crops and what wives need for their houses. I pushed that cart—in the year 1871, mind you—I pushed that cart West. Well, I took the train to Omaha, but after that I was on foot pushing it every day of the year.

"And I'm telling you, it was a good life. I was young and strong and wondering what I could do in this world. That cart gave me my living and adventure, both. I pushed from farm to farm, ranch to ranch through Nebraska and Dakota, Wyoming, Colorado, Kansas, Texas, staying ahead of the season, warm in winter, not too hot in summer. Every day was tough, but every day I sold something. Once I even sold harness to the Comanche. They thought I was their prisoner, but I made them my customers. But that's another story.

"You don't know that country, young man? Bigger than you can imagine, and empty! Skinned to the bone. But scattered over it are these brave men and women who pull a living out of the earth without help from anybody. They do without, live years, if they have to, in a house buried in the ground under a sod roof, while the sun bakes them and blizzards blow. But they're proud people, and there's no turning back.

"At night, when they're sitting at the fire with a guest—I found hospitality most every night—they talk, talk about where they come from, about their people. And you know what, young man? They come from kings."

"*Kings?*"

"Well, maybe they do, maybe they don't, Reverend, but they like to think they do. In a sod house with a cow in the corner, the wind howling, she's talking about how her grandfather was cheated out of his land, or how crooks stole the family business—how, but for some old injustice, they'd be rich. The husband lets her prattle on, or joins in with legends of his own. Where's the harm?

"I heard a lot of such stories, Reverend, but one particular one I heard over and over: How in New York before the Revolutionary War, a family had a farm, but after the war had it no longer, for a gang of thieves in clerical collars stole it, and now that farm's the priceless heart of the city.

"This story I heard while wolves sang and hailstones pounded. Once a twister rushed up and we jumped into a root cellar, and the whole history of the Slaughter farm tumbled out of a woman's bitter mouth.

"I tell you, young man, stories can keep a family going. Those families shivering with the American Dream kept going. But me they inspired, and when I finally got tired of pushing that cart—and in your thirties, some things you get tired of—I came back to Brooklyn.

"Tell me, my boy, what *is* the American Dream, really, but to find some sucker to sell it to? *Hmmm?*

"From that time to this, I make my living very simply: I write you a letter telling you you're an heir to the Slaughter farm, that at last the family's going to law with—in the opinion of their fancy-pants attorneys—excellent prospects, and invite you to chip in if you want your share. If your name's Smith or Johnson, I mention the Slaughters adopted a boy named Smith and left everything to him, or that Mrs. Slaughter's maiden name was Johnson."

"Smith or Johnson?"

"Or Stackpole, their only child married a Stackpole! I'd

write Smiths in Texas, say. A few dollars for a chance at *millions?* Better than a sweepstakes! They'd send in their money, then get busy writing Aunt Sallie Smith and Cousin Lou Smith, and they'd send money, too, *begging* to join the suit."

"You made a living from that?"

"A good one! My late brother, Richie's father, I brought in with me. We'd hold meetings in Lubbock or Wichita Falls, fifty cousins would come to town, or a hundred. We'd tell them how good things were looking, how confident the lawyers were—my brother had the manner, he was a lawyer when needed—how justice was coming at long last. 'Up to *you* how to split your billion, just pay our fees. Hundred dollars from each will make you millionaires.' Oh, the cash would fly. And for the hope it gave them, cheap at the price.

"My brother died a few years ago, and I brought Richie into the business. Won't hide from you, I was worried. He looks about as tough as a girl.

"He pulled this Denton Slaughter's name out of some farm directory and wrote him. But when this farmer who bore the royal name itself packed up his daughter and came all the way from Kansas, I thought we were through, I did indeed. But *Richie!*" Weis threw back his head and laughed until a bailiff frowned our way. "Richie saw just how to play it.

"Tell you this, Reverend, *I* don't feel sorry for the Slaughters. Lucky not to be hanged for supporting the British! But there's no limit to what people want, you know."

"Doctoring evidence wasn't part of your scheme?"

"No, my boy, never! Just as it never occurred to *me* actually to go to court! But my nephew, he's a genius." He chuckled as the bailiff looked bloody murder at us. "For me this business was good—better than pushing a cart. But my nephew's born here, him small potatoes do not interest."

"He prefers prison?"

"*What* prison? My nephew wants to work on Wall Street. Believe me, on the Street he would soon be Number One. Denton Slaughter was his 'fall guy,' but *you—you* were a *godsend*. Don't worry, you're not going anywhere either, your people will take care of you. But my advice? Don't let them laugh at their *Rover Boy* any more. Time you did a *Horatio Alger,* made something of yourself."

"Thank you, Mr. Weis."

The bailiffs fanned out to recall everybody and, as I got up to return to my seat, someone plucked at my sleeve. It was Hopkins of *The World*.

"Listen, Reverend, you did the best you could, but doesn't the Bible tell us justice isn't for this world?"

No sooner had he kindly delivered this than Weis and Seyforth and the rest came back into the courtroom. To my surprise, Shoatsbury took a seat at Whitehouse's table.

"All rise!"

Judge Gerard entered.

"Well, Mr. Seyforth, Mr. Whitehouse," he said, "I think the matter's settled to the satisfaction of the parties?"

"Yes, Your Honor," said Seyforth. "And we thank Your Honor and Mr. Whitehouse for forbearing to refer Father Stackpole's perjury for prosecution."

"Mr. Whitehouse, what say you in open court?"

"We're satisfied, Your Honor."

"Then I think, for the record, we should hear from Mr. Richard Weis."

Weis took the witness stand and was sworn.

The judge addressed him: "Mr. Weis, do you admit to violating New York State Criminal Code sections 881-883 by uttering that forgery"—he paused to take a breath—"attached as Exhibit 'A' to the amended complaint in *Slaughter versus All*

Angels Church?"

"Yes, Your Honor," said Weis.

"Mr. Seyforth, what say you?" asked the judge. "Ought the People bind Mr. Weis over for prosecution?"

Seyforth suggesting that he address his question to the distinguished Warden of All Angels, Judge Gerard asked, "Mr. Shoatsbury, what say you?"

Shoatsbury propped himself up on the flattened tips of his sausage fingers and rumbled, "Do as you will, Your Honor, only I would request that you remand Mr. Weis to *my* custody. As we discussed in chambers, although his—*um*—*scheme* to steal property worth a billion dollars was—*um*—*wrong*, the ingenuity and energy he displayed in carrying out his—*um*—*plot* were altogether admirable! And his candor and forthrightness in confessing to it equally—*um*—*remarkable*.

"These qualities have made a favorable impression on me. Accordingly, to repeat what I said in chambers, thinking mercy rather than punishment will better conduce to the—*um*—*rehabilitation* of his character, I wish to offer Mr. Weis a job with my firm, Shoatsbury & Co."

"Mr. Weis," asked the judge, "do you accept Mr. Shoatsbury's offer?"

"I do, Your Honor," said Weis.

Seyforth stood up. "Your Honor, I move for summary judgment dismissing this action with prejudice."

"Mr. Whitehouse? Any objection?"

"No, Your Honor."

"Very well, I hereby dismiss with prejudice *Slaughter versus All Angels Church*."

The gavel came down and a bailiff barked, "All rise."

"Your Honor!" roared Denton Slaughter from the back. "Your Honor, this is an outrage! We want *justice*! Weis, tell them! *Tell* them how All Angels is thieves dressed up as priests! Judge, we came here for *justice!*"

He tried to launch himself over the benches. Bailiffs had to escort him out of the courtroom. I thought I saw froth bubbling at his mouth.

Delia headed my way.

"Delia," I appealed, "let me explain—"

She didn't even look at me as she said in passing, "Pathetic boy, I never want to see you again." Going up to Weis, she laid a slap square on his cheek with what sounded like, "*Cad!* My heart you can steal, but you dare betray my *father?*"

White-faced, she turned to walk away but dropped to the floor in a faint. She was instantly attended to; I could not penetrate to her. My blushing doppelgängers got busy loading Seyforth's briefcases. Seyforth snapped one shut with a prim squeeze of his lips.

Naturally I wished to speak with Weis. He was scanning the room when I reached him.

"Weis—" I began.

Looking past me, he absolutely tried to walk through my body as though I weren't there. When that didn't work, he stepped around me, jostling his uncle also. Ignoring his uncle's outstretched hand, he hastened after the departing hogback of his new boss.

CODA

THE REST, SAVE FOR my glorious personal fate, is dismal anticlimax.

After Judge Gerard's hearing I delayed my return to the rectory almost to the close of day. First, intuiting I was to take leave of it, I took a long walk through All Angels' demesne. Once upon a time, passing amidst the skyscrapers, stores, wharves, mansions and apartment houses that paid their rent to the parish put a seigniorial spring in my step. That day I trudged, even after sprightly showers began to fall.

The headlines of *The World*'s extra edition proclaimed:

Angels Sing!
Farmer's Forgery Exposed
"Rover Boy" Lies on Stand!
Priest's Perjury Boots Rube!

I didn't buy a copy.

The moment that, wet, exhausted, hungry and sorrier than I could say, I came through the door, Mrs. Brown informed me that Father Day wished to see me. I was permitted to knock at his office door by the large and fresh-faced young priest who sat at my old desk. I had never seen him before. Unmistakably he smirked at me.

"Come in!" the rector called. I went in. Without raising his head from the blueprints he was studying, he said with a smacking sound, "Sit down, Father Stackpole."

While waiting I looked through his open windows down Wall Street to Federal Hall, where George Washington in larger-than-life-size bronze was dispensing benedictions to the stock market. It had just closed, and men in black coats and hats carrying black umbrellas hustled over the sidewalks in a sea of conflict. Some that day had won; jumps in the value of their shares put a cheerfulness in their acceptance of the rain. Others took their drenching before vanishing down subway entrances like leaves in a storm drain.

Father Day finally leaned back, screwed up his mouth and appeared to focus slightly in front of me.

"Albert, I cannot express how disappointed in you I am."

"I'm sorry, Father Day, I hoped I was helping justice prevail, but—"

"—but you find you were an instrument of the devil instead," he finished for me. "I want you to go out to St. Anselm's. Everything's arranged."

St. Anselm's is a retreat house on a Westchester County hilltop.

"But my duties here—"

"—shall be attended to. Did you meet Father Butler on your way in? Mrs. Brown's packed your bag, and a cab's waiting to take you to the station. There's a train on the hour."

"*Oh.* Very well. Father Day, I want to thank you for everything—"

"Albert, you cannot live your whole life as a promising young man." With this Delphic utterance—amounting, I think, pretty much to what old Weis had told me—he rocked his chair forward and extended a limp hand. I shook it as he spoke a final word: *"Hurry."*

During my ride to the sloppy construction site of the new Grand Central Terminal, the sky cleared and the setting sun burned orange hieroglyphics in the eastern sky.

Retreat is a Romish idea—examining one's conscience while roaming forest paths or contemplating gardens, eating spare meals, going to sleep at sunset on a hard bed and rising at dawn. Such a regime helps clear a man's head and presents his actions to him in their true light.

Gradually, in the days that followed, my soreness was assuaged as I came to accept that I *had* been an instrument of evil; unwittingly, to be sure, and with the very best intentions. I felt manipulated by all sides. If I were such a buccaneer as the rector, I might have been proof against such efforts. But my nature was different. My nature required submission to a more spiritual way, to unchanging verities and age-old ritual. These, I considered, were not to be found in the real-estate wing of a church founded to facilitate a king's divorce.

I stayed some three weeks at St. Anselm's. My last day, a Sunday, we penitents as a treat were trundled to Holy Eucharist at St. Mathew's in Bedford Village. The service was high, but failed to satisfy. With eyes refreshed by rest and reflection, I saw Episcopal trappings lavished atop a thin gruel of liturgy.

Later they set me down at the Katonah train station. My destination was Pawling, at whose new school I was to teach mathematics. I was waiting on the platform with a companion who had a similar assignment when, at an inner urging I could not but obey, I abruptly shook his hand, said goodbye and walked off.

Carrying my suitcase away from the station, going I knew

not whither, I happened to glance up and see a clapboard church raising a cross against a hillside.

I walked uphill to St. Andrew's Roman Catholic Church and went inside. Immediately I knew I was home. Mass was being sung in Latin—High Mass. Incense filled the air; from the altar came flashes of silver and crystal as the priest's nimble fingers worked wine to blood, bread to flesh. I fell to my knees.

Afterwards I approached good Father Murphy and asked for instruction. In due course he baptized me at his hideous font, and soon I was at seminary again, up the Hudson. There was born my special devotion to Mary, the amiable, beautiful, virgin Mother of God. Eventually, having taken the required vows—and after the bewilderments, betrayals and frustrations of courtship, pledging myself to chastity felt like pulling on comfortable old clothes—I was ordained a Roman Catholic priest and entered upon my humble, penitential, transcendental duties as assistant at St. Gertrude's in Utica.

The after-echoes of Denton Slaughter's attempt to claim his inheritance have been muted. His story appears to have vanished into the maw of New York's appetite for novelty, to become another of its arcane and little-visited legends. But I do know his fate.

After the court hearing, he returned to the Fifth Avenue Hotel and, seized by a spirit of reciprocity, commanded a banquet in Mrs. Astor's honor. Preparations were made, Delmonico's hired and invitations engraved, but one bill happened to be sent in early, and that bill brought down the House of Slaughter. He couldn't pay it. It may only have been for the floral centerpieces, but he couldn't pay it and became truculent, waving a cigar about his reception room and talking wildly about the Civil War and Confederate cannons.

The police were called, Slaughter's agitation increased, he

struck an officer. He was arrested and hauled off to the precinct house on 20th Street. His bail paid by no one knows whom, he returned to the hotel, only to find his belongings piled on the sidewalk, an enormous bill pinned to them. With Delia's help he ferried them a block to the Chelsea Hotel. At the end of the week, a bill was presented for their two rooms there, he couldn't pay it, the police arrived, and this time things got out of hand. For his own safety Slaughter was placed in a strait-jacket and taken to Bellevue Hospital. Later they moved him to the octagonal insane asylum on Blackwell's Island.

There he stayed. The poor man never recovered his wits, but raved about his lost patrimony to the end of his days, days he spent forging deeds and leases and royal grants. One morning in 1923, as he was being walked for exercise, subway trains clanking overhead on the Queensborough Bridge, he pointed to the distant pinnacle of the new Woolworth Building, the tallest in the world, and told his keepers that although the *Cathedral of Commerce* stood on land he owned, he had yet to receive even a peppercorn in rent and, becoming agitated — his keepers mocking him, I imagine — proclaimed that they couldn't, *wouldn't* get away with it, and threw himself into the East River.

His body was not recovered, which saved it from the ignominy of a pauper's grave. The following Sunday's *Daily News* published old photographs of him whose harsh rotogravure revealed what one had missed in life — the man's sheer delusionary fanaticism.

With him went perhaps the best opportunity of penetrating to the truth about the fabulous Slaughter Estate, which now seems doomed to remain obscure. Every few years I read about yet another attempt at it, pressed by supposed heirs of almost infinite remove, but they never get anywhere. All

Angels bats them away like so many gnats.

My impression had been that Delia Slaughter returned to Kansas to live on the remnants of her father's property. But several years after the lawsuit's dismissal, when I was in town to buy some sacred article or other, I happened to run into a former diocesan acquaintance whose account differed. He had it that in November following the events I've narrated, Delia, carrying an infant in her arms, trekked through an early snowstorm to the Maternity Hospital on Second Avenue and passed the child through the wall into the crib provided there for babies whose mothers wish to give them up for adoption, and that, coming away again, she accosted a stranger and walked off with him.

This story I doubt; I believe my friend felt an unconscious resentment of my (so to say) apostasy and that it owes its purported facts to that cause. As I've seen too often in my subsequent career, although a mother may give up her newborn at birth, she'll never summon the strength to do so later; but neither will a woman who's just given birth go with a man. So this supposed sighting I put down to the kind of mythmaking New York lends itself to. I prefer to believe that Delia Slaughter indeed returned to Kansas and has been married these 30 years to some respectable son of the soil to whom she's borne half a dozen handsome children.

Whatever the facts of her fate, I do not blame Delia. If she pretended to feel more affection for me than she actually felt, that was perhaps part of her own temptation.

Bishop Day, as he became after so masterfully negotiating the Woolworth Building's ground lease, long occupied a mansion on the grounds of St. John the Divine. He was much loved for the interest he took in New York's young street toughs, whatever their religion or nationality. He stood bail, provided lawyers, gave job referrals, was always ready to whisper surety into a judge's ear or provide a bed to sleep in. The boys, in turn, worshipped him, vying to kneel and kiss his ring.

His death came in 1929, on the Wednesday before Black Tuesday. Alas, one cannot credit his impeccable market timing: He was bludgeoned by a young thug to whom he was endeavoring to give succor. His funeral the day the stock market crashed brought out his "boys" from throughout the region, most of them now solid middle-aged businessmen. Also in attendance was the Vestry of All Angels, and I still wonder whether having so many Wall Street potentates away from their desks that morning contributed to the Crash. His coffin, pulled by white horses to a tomb carved with skyscrapers in Uptown Angels Cemetery, was accompanied by a corps of youths from Bishop Day Academy ringing silver hand bells.

I shall never forget those gorgeous tones tolling him to his rest. The electric chair speeded his killer to his own.

Bishop Day's successors at All Angels have increased its wealth and influence beyond reckoning, and also raised the neighborhood quite a bit nearer heaven. The present rector has restored the church, replacing Stanford White's old-fashioned additions with the admirable modern Mediterranean tile and wrought iron of Mott B. Schmidt. The baptismal font remains, however.

As to old Weis's fate, I have no information, but his nephew Richard Weis is, of course, the principal of Shoatsbury, Weis & Co. and one of the city's leading citizens. Shoatsbury assigned him first to trade pork bellies in the pit where men do battle with degrading gestures of appetite. Weis apparently coming away with more pork bellies than anybody else, Shoatsbury brought him into the office and made him an all-around master of finance, and not long before his own tragic demise (choking at a banquet for his beloved Unfortunates of the Streets) his full partner.

Shoatsbury, Weis operates out of the Georgian tower Weis built on Exchange Place. It underwrites bond offerings from the biggest corporations and safest municipalities; in addition, Weis chairs the bond committees of numerous overseas railways. He and his wife, heiress to a divagation of the Phipps fortune, donate fabulous sums to museums and medical research, and the angel faces of their brood frequently grace the society pages. And not only has Weis long been a communicant of All Angels Church, for several years past he has served as its Warden.

As for me, it's been my privilege this past decade to be pastor of St. Ladislaus, a fine Polish-Irish parish in Greenpoint, Brooklyn. Here I do plain daily labor in a vineyard of souls; I need never look at a lease or deal with irritable titans of finance. Poverty roosts permanently in this neighborhood, and yet good people live here. (I find that money and virtue, although not absolutely incompatible, are by no means the brethren of Father Day's imagination.)

On any given day I might carry to the hospital an old lady who can no longer care for herself, much less for her 40 cats; counsel a girl whose distended belly shows I'm many months too late; offer advice to a married couple, he a sullen dockworker, she a worn housewife with two black eyes; help a lad find the work his probation requires; serve soup to the hungry lined up around the block, in addition to saying Mass and my office, hearing confessions, performing baptisms and last rites, presiding at weddings and funerals.

Occasionally, I look across the river at the skyscrapers marching up Manhattan Island. Sometimes I even remember that once I had something to do with them.

Then I get back to work.

www.ingramcontent.com/pod-product-compliance
Lightning Source LLC
LaVergne TN
LVHW091547060526
838200LV00036B/732